"Wayne Elsey has dedicated his life to making a difference through the organization Soles4Souls, and millions of people have shoes on their feet because of that dedication. *Almost Isn't Good Enough* is a great read for people who think they are too insignificant to do something great in life."

—Antawn Jamison
NBA Cleveland Cavaliers

"Soles4Souls is a significant organization making a real difference in the lives of people around the world, and it is led by a friend who knows the importance of giving back. His book, *Almost Isn't Good Enough*, is a perfect example of how anyone can use their influence to incite positive change in the world."

—Jeff Fisher
Former NFL Head Coach of the Tennessee Titans

"Footwear is an important part of our business, but for millions of children around the world it is the missing puzzle piece for their health and well-being. Soles4Souls and Wayne Elsey have become a shining light in the bleak and overwhelming reality of global poverty today. *Almost Isn't Good Enough* is an encouraging, uncomplicated example of how to make your life count."

—Scott Sessa
President of Minnetonka

"Of Wayne's many successes, Soles4Souls has been his ultimate inspiration and masterpiece. *Almost Isn't Good Enough* is pure Wayne and a must-read for those who want insight into this remarkable achievement."

—David DiPasquale
Industry Executive and Long-Time Friend

"I have always believed in the mission of Soles4Souls. Their determination and focus to make a dent in the staggering number of children without shoes is inspiring and has forced the footwear industry to action. *Almost Isn't Good Enough* is a fool-proof guide to how one life can make a difference around the world."

—Evan Cagner
President of BCNY International / Synclaire Brands

"Wayne Elsey is a visionary in the footwear industry who has used his many talents and passion for helping others to touch the lives of millions who are benefitting from the work of Soles4Souls. I am proud to call him a friend."

—Tim O'Donovan
Retired Chairman and CEO of Wolverine World Wide, Inc.

"*Almost Isn't Good Enough* is a simple, straightforward guide to not allowing others' expectations define your life. Wayne Elsey speaks the truth about how one life and one decision can help change the world."

—Andy Andrews
New York Times *bestselling author of* **The Traveler's Gift**

"As a successful global company, SKECHERS believes it is our duty, and honor, to help those less fortunate around the world—be it through hundreds of thousands of shoes or raising funds to support education and special needs children."

—Michael Greenberg
President of SKECHERS

"I believe the phrase used often by Wayne and the title of this book, *Almost Isn't Good Enough*, will become a coined phrase in the near future. This book inspires the reader to evaluate past experiences and opportunities and ask, 'Did I do enough?' It challenges, encourages, and provides one the tools to make an impactful difference in his or her own life and the lives of others."

—**Connie Elder**
Founder/CEO of Connie Elder International

"*Almost Isn't Good Enough* is a road map for individuals, young and old, looking to inspire a positive change in their corner of the world. Millions of people have been impacted through the incredible generosity and mission of Soles4Souls. Wayne's enthusiasm and passion have helped steer the footwear industry toward a more altruistic outlook on the world."

—**Diane Sullivan**
President, COO, and Director, Brown Shoe Company, Inc.

"Wayne Elsey's engrossing *Almost Isn't Good Enough* tells the story of a passionate man and his one-of-a-kind mission. Along the way, the reader gets some intriguing insights about the entrepreneurial spirit, management strategy, and the complicated yet fascinating world of philanthropy. This is a book that anyone can learn some important life lessons from."

—**Michael Atmore**
Editorial Director, **Footwear News**

"Soles4Souls was a bold step by one man with the vision, the desire, clearly the need, and the inside knowledge of what the American boot and shoe business could deliver on."

—**Mike Brooks**
CEO of Rocky Brands

Almost Isn't Good Enough

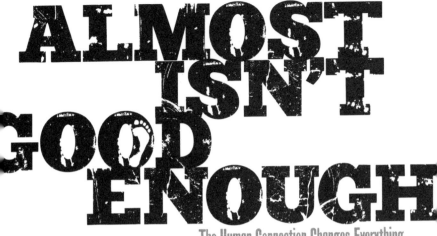

ALMOST ISN'T GOOD ENOUGH

The Human Connection Changes Everything

Wayne Elsey
Founder and CEO of Soles4Souls

Changing the World
Publishing

NASHVILLE

Published in Nashville, Tennessee, by Changing the World Publishing, 319 Martingale Dr., Old Hickory, Tennessee 37138

Printed in the United States of America

11 10   1 2

ISBN (HC): 978-1-4507-4123-1
ISBN (TP): 978-1-4507-4124-8

Library of Congress Control Number: 2011923258.

Grafix Design Studio
Nashville, Tennessee
www.grafixdesignstudio.net

To my daughter, Melissa,
who rocks my world every day
with her beauty, laughter,
giving heart, and sarcasm.

CONTENTS

It's important to be simple and clear about your objectives and goals. The goal of Soles4Souls is to put shoes on the feet of people without shoes. That absolute clarity helps the brand resonate with donors and clarifies organizational decision making.

Acknowledgments

I consider myself to be one of the luckiest people in the world. There is nothing greater to achieve in life than to love and be loved. I'm grateful I have both. I wanted to take the opportunity to honor a few special people who have made an unforgettable and undeniable mark on my life.

Melissa Elsey, you rock! I know you struggle because we look so much alike, act alike, and are just alike. I hope I inspire you. Even though I'm just a simple guy and an imperfect father, I have always loved you and will always be your biggest fan. I love you more than anything in the world. You can do anything you want if you put your mind to it. I am so proud of you!

Mathias and Virginia Elsey, thank you for being parents with a cause. You guys provided a great start to my life and always made sure my needs were met.

Timmy Elsey, my late brother, your legacy continues in me today. Thank you for all you did to help shape the man

I have become. You were a great brother and an awesome guy. You would be so proud of your daughter, Crystal. She reminds me so much of you.

John McLendon, a pastor and friend. You are a very real guy. I think that's why I totally enjoy our time together. I love your strategy of doing church, reaching out to imperfect people that are five feet away from hell instead of perfect people. I wish more pastors were like you. Keep fighting the good fight!

Tiffany Johnson, you know how much I love you. You are inspiring, motivating, and full of life. Thank you for sharing your life with me.

Jackie Busch, thank you for believing in me, lighting my fire, and saving my life. You gave me permission to follow my heart. I've been doing so ever since.

Bob Busch, how many flags did we collect that day? I will never forget doing that along with your terrible choice of used cars.

Fran Venincasa, you are the coolest guy I have ever met. I have learned a lot from you. Thanks for reminding me how important it is to send flowers to the people we choose to do life with. Also, you are the only person that I've ever met that is older than their in-laws. Amazing!

Kathy Hamelin, you are a saint and one of the nicest people ever.

Connie Elder, my buddy, we have always been real with each other and not afraid to just say it like it is. That is so important to me!

Nelson Wilson, thanks for your heart. You're my favorite dentist. I'm grateful that you have your heart on display via the pictures displayed throughout your office. And thanks for taking the pictures of me using a fork lift and dolly. Priceless.

Genevieve (Chickie) Lazzara, I love all the names you call me when I beat you at cards, which is most of the time. I also love your eggplant. Thanks for being you!

Joelle Dalton, thanks for your tireless volunteer contribution and getting the need for shoes during the initial stages.

John Ortberg, you have inspired me through the years. I am proud to be in your circle of friends. Your authenticity motivates me. Thanks for being a great friend.

Dan Pallotta, you wrote the book, literally, on the changing dynamics of nonprofit work. Thanks for giving me a map and a vocabulary for doing this work differently. Also, grateful for our friendship.

Ben Stroup, thanks for your partnership in developing this book. I loved watching the process unfold from an idea to a finished product. Without you, this would never have happened.

A big thanks to my team at Soles4Souls, both past and present. You are leading people, developing strategies, and achieving measurable results that are changing lives every day. It is a privilege to do this work with you. Thanks for getting us where we are today. I'm excited about what's next. We have just begun!

Finally, those to whom we have given shoes: I wish you the best. Never forget a pair of shoes brings hope. I hope you never forget to go for it! There is a better tomorrow.

Foreword

This amazing book is part blueprint for running a 21st century humanitarian organization operating on the power of daring 21st century ideas, and part personal inspiration manifesto.

In *Uncharitable*, I wrote about the religious edifice we have come to glorify as the nonprofit "ethic"—an ethic which I believe seriously undermines our ability to create meaningful change in the world. This ethic encourages cultures of deprivation in charity and discourages charities from doing all of the things it would take to actually make good on their missions—for example, hiring the best people and paying them market rates to keep and incentivize them, taking risks to achieve more mission, thinking long-term, and investing money in the strength of the organization. The last chapter in my book is about the need for humanitarian sector leaders to step forward—stick their necks out—and challenge these irrational, 400-year-old operating norms.

Soles4Souls has its neck out in a big way. And it's totally inspiring. It is an example of an organization that is, every day, demonstrating the kind of courage I challenged people to call forth. It's a trail-blazing initiative doing things in brand new ways, rejecting obsolete operating paradigms—no matter how sacred—that get in the way of producing real results for real people in need. It takes business risks, it hires the best people and pays them well, it pays more attention to the good it's doing than to what the media thinks, it educates its donors instead of cowering before them, it thinks long-term, and it's focused on impact all the way down the line.

Soles4Souls is wildly successful, and stands as a model to other nonprofits. Why is it a model? Because it upholds the highest ethical standards. It has none of the conflict of interest between mission and public relations that is the hallmark of many large nonprofits. Soles4Souls honestly earns the right to its tax-exempt status—not just by offering tax-deductibility on donations, which is the limit of what many others do—but by maintaining an uncompromising and uncompromisable commitment to mission over institutional aggrandizement. In other words, it puts people who are hurting first. And my guess is that's what they want.

In the pages ahead you'll see exactly how they're doing that. You'll read frank, unequivocal advice that you're not going to see in other books on the sector—things like, "don't listen to anyone or let anything distract you from where you want to go," "absolute clarity is the key to unlocking the complex nature of business," "a distracted life is an unsatisfied life," "cash is king," and "hire the best and pay the best." And you'll also find hard-hitting analysis that says things like, "that is crazy!" I did not add the exclamation point.

You know how I met Wayne Elsey? He called me. On a Sunday afternoon, in my office. I don't know how he tracked down my phone number or what made him decide I might be around on a Sunday afternoon or why he didn't choose to e-mail me instead, like everyone else does these days. He just called me. I was there, I picked up, we spoke, and realized immediately that we had common ideas about making a difference in the world and could be supportive and helpful to one another.

And that says pretty much everything about Wayne and about the value awaiting you in the pages ahead. He's a man of action. He doesn't sit around over-thinking things, plotting chess outcomes nine moves down the line, or worrying about failure or rejection. He acts. And acts. And acts. And acts. It's a way of being for him. He can't *not* act. It's not in his blood. And it's good to get exposed to someone like that. This book will do just that. It will put you in Wayne's reality, and you'll get to see things in that reality that you may not have thought possible in your own.

What you're about to read isn't Shakespeare or *War and Peace*. It ain't difficult to understand. It's plain-spoken, thank God. And it's not high-minded academic theory calculated to win a Pulitzer or a Nobel. But, if you're like me, you'll find yourself unable to put the book down. Why? Because here is, in the raw, a real social entrepreneur. A real live, accomplished, successful, social entrepreneur, with the results to prove it. Here is an Evel Knievel for social change. Not a pontificator. Not a theoretician. Not a talking head. Not someone who thinks about things all day long and packages his thinking in a framework of new buzzwords, without any track record or life achievement to back the damned thing up. Here's a real, honest-to-goodness person who, with the amazing team he has put together, actually achieves things. Produces results. Consistently.

And he jumps out of the pages at you.

Almost Isn't Good Enough is packed fresh with Wayne's extraordinary capacity for personal openness and vulnerability, which gives the entire read wonderful strength and beauty. It's also full of contrarian ideas, which separates it from the mountain of books out there about the nonprofit sector and social change that are pregnant with caution. This is what gives the book its real value. You won't come away with nothing here. You won't come away being unable to figure out what you were supposed to have come away with.

The voice of this book is strong and opinionated. It's a voice and opinion that point the way to something refreshingly unabstract: helping people who suffer not to suffer anymore. In the end, that's what the high-fallutin' notion of "change the world" is really all about.

—**Dan Pallotta**
Author of **Uncharitable,** *founder of Pallotta TeamWorks,*
president of Springboard, nonprofit sector innovator,
and social entrepreneur

preface

There is a line in one of the prophets that haunts the reader: "How beautiful on the mountain are the feet of those who bring good news." Feet were not generally considered beautiful in the ancient world. They were not big into sidewalks, which meant everybody's feet were constantly being covered with mud and dirt and worse. Washing feet was menial labor, a job for slaves. Jesus washed feet. Jesus was the one who carried good news. Jesus had beautiful feet.

In our day, where I live, people don't give a lot of thought to feet, or to shoes for that matter (outside of *Sex and the City* fans). I had always more or less taken them for granted. That is, until I met Wayne.

Wayne Elsey, for those of you who have not yet had the fortune of meeting him, is one of those larger-than-life characters. The story of his rise to success in the shoe industry with (to say the least) not much experience is something out of a movie. The story of how, as a young boy, he came to discover that he might have something worthwhile to offer to the world, enough to stick around for a few more years, is even more riveting.

But the most compelling thing about Wayne is not Wayne. It's feet.

In one of those unlikely, I-was-not-looking-for-it moments, somebody spoke to Wayne. Somebody who cares about the poor was going to ask Wayne to make a difference and give him a passion and sense of meaning to boot. (Slight footwear pun, I know.) Somebody who sounded suspiciously like God, if God can use a TV to speak to somebody.

And Wayne went from being a man with a resume to a man with a mission. He did not lose any of his old fire, drive, impatience, or demand for results. Instead, he channeled all that energy toward the enhancement of human beings who do not have enough money for a simple pair of shoes and are left with the risk of infection, disease, discomfort, disfigurement, or any number of conditions that those of us who are easily-shod never have to think about.

You have a chance to "meet" Wayne in this book. I want you to imagine that you are talking with a soft-spoken, well-heeled, carefully coiffed man who looks exactly like George Clooney. Only, you should know that Wayne is nothing like the image in your mind right now.

Meeting Wayne means getting a scent of the passion that drives him, and you can't get a whiff of it without wanting some yourself. But, if he were speaking to you right now, he would tell you that what matters is not that you meet him. His story is not really his story, after all.

What matters is that maybe, just maybe, the same One who spoke to Wayne some time ago about the suffering and hurting and lacking in this world might speak through Wayne to you as well. And maybe your life will become larger than your life too.

It's about the shoes, but it's really not about the shoes. It's about the people who wear them.

–John Ortberg
Senior pastor of Menlo Park Presbyterian Church, speaker, and author of numerous books such as When the Game Is Over, It All Goes Back in the Box; The Life You've Always Wanted; *and* The Me I Want to Be

Introduction:
Shoe is a Four-Letter Word ... So is Hope

I remember the first time I stepped into Mrs. Busch's classroom. It was my sophomore year of high school, and she was my homeroom teacher. Mrs. Busch had already been teaching nearly a decade by the time our paths intersected. I immediately knew something was different about her.

I'll never forget this one girl in our class who was constantly late to school. School policy called for a suspension after collecting three tardies, and there was no room for interpretation. This girl was due to feel the full weight of her circumstance when Mrs. Busch slid a quarter across her student desk and suggested she call her mother to inform the school that her tardiness was due to not feeling well. This girl didn't immediately connect the dots. In fact, it took my classmate hearing Mrs. Busch's suggestion three times before fully understanding the compassionate plea and redemptive opportunity that was being provided to her.

Mrs. Busch cared about her students. More importantly, she cared about me.

A Haunting Accusation

I was a teenager tired of school and ready to graduate. Screaming for my own identity and sense of self, I never really felt like I fit anywhere. I was tall, lanky, and felt forgotten and overlooked. Raised in a blended family, I was the youngest of four. I had many friends and was well-liked, so I don't mean to suggest that I was a recluse or anti-social.

Still, those teenage years are full of self-doubt, overcome with questions, and fueled by a level of energy that can hardly be contained within the confines of home and school. For me, it didn't help when one teacher told me I wouldn't amount to anything. I don't remember all the details surrounding the event, but I can hear those words as clearly today as I did back then.

We have little idea how what we say affects others. He never knew it, but his accusation would haunt me for years to come. I was determined to prove him wrong.

I remember one time in particular when I was struggling to discern up from down. It was one of those days when nothing seemed to be going right and every turn delivered another unanticipated and unwelcomed surprise. Mrs. Busch knew something was bothering me. She was very perceptive and easily read between the lines.

We talked, and I told her everything. I'll never forget what she said: "Wayne, you can do anything you want to do. Just do it."

That was the first time in my life someone told me I could

do whatever I wanted to do. Finally, I was given permission to dream big and make something happen. Mrs. Busch's words resonated within me and fueled my desire to prove wrong the other teacher and every critic of mine going forward.

You Can Do Anything You Want to Do

Those words may not seem special or extraordinary, but they became the cadence of my career. So from an early age, I felt empowered knowing that what was most important was my decision to take action and do something rather than sit, wait, think, and plan. My willingness to work hard—not what others allowed me to do—would turn my dreams into reality.

I remember selling fruitcakes in the subways of Washington, D.C. The 4-H club was selling each fruitcake for four dollars. I determined they were highly undervaluing the product, so I decided to sell the same fruitcakes for five dollars. I sold every fruitcake I could get my hands on that day. The exact amount of profit escapes me now, but I do know I was the only student who actually turned a profit on fruitcakes.

I didn't always make good choices. I still had to learn that every decision has a corresponding consequence. The same Mrs. Busch who unleashed my potential also gave me my first zero in class. I deserved it.

Let's just say I was tired from not sleeping much the night before, so I found a place to take a nap during one four-hour summer school class. When I awoke, I realized I had slept through the entire class. After the other students were dismissed, I asked Mrs. Busch if I could make up what I had missed. She told me no because the reason I missed was a result of my decision, not hers. With a lot of hard work, I was still able to make an A in the class.

I believe Mrs. Busch wanted me to learn that my decisions will take me where I want to go. Her wisdom would later prove invaluable.

First Steps in the Footwear Industry

School was never difficult for me, but I wasn't a bookworm. I couldn't wait to graduate and be in the real world. Thankfully, I was part of a school-sponsored program that let me go to school for a half-day and work the other half-day. That's when I started in the shoe business. It was my first step into the industry that would shape my life.

I was only fifteen at the time, but I ran the local shoe store in town. I wasn't officially the manager, because I was a minor. Functionally, though, there wasn't a difference. I knew I was good at what I did. I never had trouble connecting with my customers, and I strived for everyone to feel as if they were the most important person in the world. It didn't matter if they were rich or poor, black or white, young or old . . . if they needed shoes, I was going to give them the best shoe experience ever. I would always sell more shoes than any other associate in the store because I didn't see a sale but a person in need.

Selling shoes to women, I learned, was a lesson in the importance of knowing your customer. Women have different shoe-shopping habits than men. They often shop together. And they value small feet. It didn't take me long to become accurate at judging the size of a woman's foot without having to measure. When a customer would shop with her friends in my store, I would always grab the correct size, which was often much larger than desired, but place the pair of shoes into a box marked with a much smaller size. The customer would know it, but her friends never noticed. Selling shoes was a mere transaction. What mattered most is that I made her feel special. I didn't provide just shoes for her to wear; I built her self-esteem and offered her a sense of dignity.

People Matter

Treating the individuals who walked through the doors of my store as human beings rather than just prospects was a practice that propelled me to consistent growth in shoe sales and accelerated my career within the industry. I wish I could take credit for this decision, but I owe it all to Mrs. Busch. It was in her class that I first saw modeled what it was like to love others unconditionally and place another's needs above my own.

Mrs. Busch would never tell this about herself, but she discretely purchased a few pairs of shoes for her students over the years. She didn't let a teacher's salary stand in the way of changing someone else's life. This bent toward helping others is why I believe we connected on so many levels. I knew that when I grew up, I wanted to be Mrs. Busch to other people. I wasn't sure exactly what that would mean, but I was certain it wasn't going to be teaching in a classroom.

Mrs. Busch is one of those people who come into your life unannounced and seemingly without cause or reason. Now I know something larger was taking place. I tried to show her how special she was to me by organizing her one (and only) student-given birthday party. Through the years we've kept in touch, and I've tried to remind her how much her words of encouragement meant to me. I once sent her and her husband to see her beloved Chicago Cubs. Another time, I flew them out to Las Vegas to join me for an event Soles4Souls was hosting. It was the least I could do.

But as for most people, my life hasn't always been full of fun, games, and success. Mrs. Busch was there for me when my brother was suddenly and unexpectedly killed. She was there when my baby girl was born three months prematurely. She was there every time I needed her, and she always told me that whatever I needed, she would help however she could.

I've told her time and again that if it wasn't for her, I am certain my life would be different. She reminds me that everything I have become and achieved was because I decided to take action and do something. Whichever version of the story is true, Mrs. Busch changed my life, and I have tried to change others lives in the same way.

One Shoe Changed Everything

Decades after high school, I found myself sitting on my couch watching the news about the terrible tsunami in Indonesia. In one TV clip, I noticed a single shoe had washed up on the beach. I felt an immediate urge and compulsion to do something to help, though I had no idea what one person could do. I may have been an executive who knew how to work the sales floor and consistently improve the bottom line—but I was a beginner when it came to charity.

I thought of Mrs. Busch and the compassion she had shown me and so many others. Her statement "You can do anything you want to do" flashed through my mind. I looked to what was most familiar: the footwear industry. It seemed like a logical place to start.

I called my friends who were also corporate executives in this small yet fiercely competitive industry in search of donations to send shoes to the survivors. Combined, we collected more than 250,000 pairs of new shoes and were able to cover the cost of shipping through monetary donations as well. I was blown away by how one act of kindness resulted in a quarter of a million shoes distributed to others in need. Judging by the surprising success of this effort, I knew I had stumbled onto something big.

Shoes are a luxury for many of us. We have multiple pairs in our closets. While most people aren't able to afford the designer names, many have the capacity to purchase a new pair of shoes at will. This is not the case for three hundred million children around the world. Some have never had a pair of shoes. Some need new shoes but can't get them. Some need the right kind of shoe to protect themselves at worksites and provide comfort and support for their demanding jobs.

The shoe business was my business. If I could organize the donation of 250,000 pairs with a few phone calls, I wondered what I might be able to do with a more organized and thoughtful effort. Starting and funding new ventures was not a new thing for me. By this time in my life, I had learned I have the ability to create something out of nothing and improve upon what already exists.

After I left the sales floor in local shoe stores, I eventually became a change agent for another, much larger shoe company. In underperforming stores, I would become their manager for a few months. I was able to turn around just about every store. This would be an invaluable skill that would carry me through what could arguably be the riskiest venture of my life: starting Soles4Souls.

It wasn't long after the Indonesian tsunami that the Katrina disaster hit New Orleans and other Gulf Coast areas. I took what I had learned and put it to work under the name Katrina Shoes. We were able to accomplish similar results with relatively little effort. It became apparent that this little operation was not going to last as a volunteer effort. I had a decision to make. I was forty years old at the time and in my peak income-earning years. I was at the top of one very well-known footwear company. Leaving my professional career behind made absolutely no sense, but I suspected from the beginning that it would be what I had to do.

My friends shared my concern and celebrated with me over the impact we already had. However, they thought I was absolutely crazy for walking away from what they believed was the job of a lifetime.

Being an executive is tough. Everything falls on your shoulders. Success and failure are yours to claim and own. There is very little about that role that isn't full of stress and expectations. It can suffocate you at times. I had proven myself as one of the best in the business, driving each and every company I led toward innovation and greater productivity and profitability. Even with every reason to leave this hobby behind, I couldn't forget the image of that single shoe I had seen on TV the day of the tsunami. I asked myself what Mrs. Busch would do. I didn't have to think long. I knew what she would have done, and I knew what I had to do. Soles4Souls had to become a full-time endeavor. It was the logical next step.

One Act of Kindness

Today, one act of kindness has become an international relief organization that has distributed more than twelve million shoes to people in need. We generate more than $75 million in contributions and hold our administrative costs to 2 percent. Our goal is to provide shoes to other people. Period. It is the simplicity of our mission and the compassion with which we do our work that I believe have set us apart from other charities and has accelerated our efforts beyond our wildest imaginations.

The reality is, you don't have to be a corporate executive turned philanthropist/nonprofit leader to make a difference in the lives of others. Though this book reveals the principles upon which I live my life and the values that have directed our decisions at Soles4Souls, everyone has the capacity to do something.

You might be a teenager filled with desires to do something that matters. You might be college student striving to understand your place in this world. You might be a young professional who quietly questions whether poring over spreadsheets and executive summaries should be the activities to which you give the best years of your life. This book is for you.

Perhaps you are a social activist, a mid-life professional looking to make a change within yourself and in the world, or even a corporate executive looking to lead your company to improve more than the bottom line. This book is for you.

However, not everyone is ready to read what is printed in this book.

If you're a pseudo-intellectual who would rather bury

yourself in statistics than look into the eyes of a human being, then this book is not for you.

If you're comfortable knowing that people around the world are suffering and you've done relatively little or nothing to leverage the margin in your life to improve someone else's life, then this book is not for you.

If you only invest in things that produce a measurable return and solely benefit you, then this book is not for you.

If you are satisfied with almost solving a problem, then stop wasting your time and put this book back on the shelf.

I'm tired of self-proclaimed, well-intentioned people settling for the life they've achieved and refusing to answer the urge that is present within each of us to connect with someone else as a human being. We were created to be loved and to do something meaningful in life. I grow weary listening to nonprofit leaders who pour donor dollars into meetings, symposiums, and informational seminars but refuse to take action. I'm tired of hearing sermons on what we should, might, or ought to do. It's time for action. It's time to gather our resources and leverage our excess to make a measurable impact. The time is now!

A Roadmap, Not a Step-by-Step Program

This book is a roadmap. It's not another leadership book that offers a step-by-step program for success. It offers key principles that have defined my personal decision making and guided my professional success as a corporate executive and as a philanthropist and nonprofit leader. While we will examine much of this paradigm shift within the context of a nonprofit organization, these principles exist beyond the walls of a corporate structure. They can be applied on an individual level too.

Each section of this book will challenge you to evaluate your current assumptions and challenge you to reorient your thinking around results, impact, and life change. Too many times charity becomes something absent of the core disciplines that make for-profit businesses successful: problem, solution, and urgency. Those same elements must be present in charity and nonprofit work. If they are missing, then one can only expect to perpetuate more of the same rather than propel others toward game-changing achievements.

A Remarkable Difference

Everyone needs a Mrs. Busch in his or her life, someone who can make a remarkable difference through a kind word or action. I have spent my life trying to impact lives in a similar way as Mrs. Busch impacted mine.

I have experienced great success in my professional life, and my success offered me the opportunity to change careers midway through my peak income-earning years. Making a difference in the life of someone else, though, is something everyone has the capacity to do regardless of where one is in life and career.

I'm not asking you to quit your job and start a nonprofit. For some, that may be the logical next step in your journey. For many, it's not practical or sound reasoning. What rings true for every person reading this is that we have more than the average person around the world, and we have the opportunity to use what we have accumulated in our closets and in our bank accounts to benefit others.

Will you join me in the battle cry of almost isn't good enough?

Will you wage war on behalf of those who are suffering, helpless, and forgotten?

It will cost you something, and the return on your investment may not be able to be cashed in for monetary value. I promise, though, that your investment will not return empty. It will create an energy around you that will attract others, change lives, and offer the opportunity to leave a legacy of change in the midst of a culture of excess.

Almost isn't good enough for me. Is it good enough for you? If not, keep reading.

Eliminate Distractions by Practicing Absolute Clarity

"Clarity affords focus."
—Thomas Leonard

Our success is a direct result of our commitment to keep our focus simple and clear. It can certainly be a challenge to maintain your focus as your momentum and capacity increases. As Soles4Souls grows, the pressure builds from within and outside the organization to diversify and broaden our focus for, as some might argue, greater impact. Our resolve must never be diverted in directions that distract us from our purpose.

Every new employee receives a laminated card that states four simple, strategic organizational goals. One of those goals is "Every day is Day 1." The description reads:

Do not forget where we started, what we have accomplished, and treat every day as Day 1.

The day I saw that single shoe wash up on the beach and felt an urge to do something to help the people most affected by such a tragic natural disaster, I had one clear goal in mind: collect and give away shoes. That simple goal, which has evolved into an international relief organization that has distributed more than twelve million shoes to people in need, is pushing us to achieve our goal of giving away one pair of shoes every second.

No one in our office has ever had to question what we are trying to accomplish, why we exist, and what should take priority. Our world headquarters also includes a distribution center. This was important to me. Many times people will stop by and drop off both small and large amounts of shoes. It doesn't matter what we are doing at the moment or the size of the donation being made—that individual and his or her donation takes top priority.

Everyone Else's Expectations

Whatever you do in life, whatever you decide to achieve, or whatever you set as your goal, there will always be someone else who will have different expectations of you. They will think you're crazy, wasting your time, or that you could do so much more. Let me give you a little advice: don't listen to anyone or let anything distract you from where you want to go.

Success, wealth, and impact are not philosophical ideas to be debated within the halls of academia. They are characteristics grounded in a focused effort over a long period of time that lead to transformation. The path to all three are not unknown; rather, they are dependent upon one person setting a course, following a plan, and executing consistently.

My best friend, Fran, was a hot-shot real estate builder and developer in the greater Boston area. He always tells me, "The secret to business is to go where the money is." While our bottom line might be different, the concept holds true. When organizations spend their efforts focusing on the greatest needs of the customer or donor, money flows freely.

You should also know that Fran thought I was absolutely crazy for leaving my corporate job. We are friends, so he has earned the right to speak freely into my life. We were sitting in the clubhouse of the condo community where I live one afternoon when I told him about this evolving project of giving away shoes to people in need. I explained to him that it was becoming much more than I could handle as a hobby.

> Simplicity enhances the ability of the leader to take action and involve more people in the effort, work, or cause.

Fran is a few years my senior and has been around the block a time or two. As a true Bostonian and full-blooded Italian, he never learned to filter what he is thinking. In a matter of seconds, he began to tell me all the reasons why I shouldn't leave my corporate career and pursue this crazy idea of a shoe charity. He was not in favor of the direction I was headed.

I appreciated his thoughts and heeded his warning. However, I knew what I had to do. I knew the direction I was headed, and I couldn't help but follow my heart. When Fran and I met again a few weeks later, I told him my decision. He said, "Figures. I knew you were going to do that." Then he smiled.

It's important to have people in your life who can test your ideas and push you to points of clarity. It's also equally important to be careful in who you allow to function in this position. Success has a strange way of attracting people who want to be successful through you. I call this success by proxy. These people end up being more of a distraction than anything else.

Campfire Discussions

Early in the life of Soles4Souls, our small team would gather together in what was then our conference room. We would go around the room and share what we were working on, what ideas we had, and where we thought the greatest opportunity for growth might be found. Since many of us were wearing multiple hats, it had been difficult to keep up with everyone.

I was already traveling and speaking as often as I was invited. This moment in our week was the only opportunity for me to hear where everyone else was investing their time and energy. It felt very much like a campfire conversation. It was as if we were sitting around a blazing fire in the dark of night and telling stories to one another.

On certain days, some ideas fit together like a square and a circle. It became evident that if we weren't careful, our initial success would wane in light of our appetite to keep growing. The greater risk was that our desperate desire to make a difference might lead us away from our core work.

I see this so often within organizations. Whether for-profit or nonprofit, organizations learn that success is a two-edged sword. It perpetuates what you are doing well, but it also increases your capacity to take on other initiatives and explore additional streams of revenue and opportunity. The greatest threat is taking on new work that doesn't support your core work, because this will distract you from what made you successful in the first place.

We had to make some changes to our campfire sessions. A critical shift in our strategy took place when we began to put together a master plan. Individuals were assigned an area of expertise that fit their own unique personalities, passions, and experience. Those leaders became the rulers of their domain. Myself, along with a few others that made up senior management, were tasked with ensuring that our new "specialists" were contributing to our larger, singularly focused objective of doing what we do best: give away shoes to people in need.

clarity is simple

Occasionally, I'm invited to consult with leaders on how to get beyond the wall that seems to be holding them back. The first thing I ask is to see their mission statement and core values. More often than not, these two items make up one or more pages of text. I lay the documents back down on the table and ask if anyone in the room can recite what's on the paper. Rarely does someone respond. The next question I ask them is an important one: If you can't recite your mission statement and core values, why do you think anyone else will be able to do so?

Leaders live closer to the details than employees, volunteers, participants, and donors. We can't assume that others understand and perceive what the leader understands and perceives. This is why it is critical to find multiple ways to tell others what you need, and this need places pressure on the leader to keep things simple. Simplicity enhances the ability of the leader to take action and involve more people in the effort, work, or cause.

Absolute clarity is the key to unlocking the complex nature of business and tapping into the energy that converts an idea to reality and transforms a hobby to an organization. From the very beginning, Soles4Souls has been about providing shoes to people in need. I have successfully kept that our main goal. Whatever other initiatives may come along, that one will remain the foundation of our organization.

The Power of "No"

Clarity gives people a sense of the desired end result and focuses their efforts in a specific direction. That means, when necessary, the leader has the confidence to say no to anything that doesn't lead the cause or organization toward the desired end result. The rule is that the bigger and more successful you become, the more difficult it is to say no.

It seems strange to suggest that there is power in saying no. I want to be careful not to sound like a Roman emperor lounging around, passively saying yes or no based on how I feel at the moment. That's not the power of "no" that I'm talking about. It's not arbitrary. I also want to be clear that tapping into the power of "no" is not an attempt to walk away from something I don't completely understand or that seems too risky. I may be a lot of things, but averse to risk is not one of them.

The power of "no" I'm talking about is a combination of

tenacity and, as some people in Tennessee say, "cussed stubbornness." It's true that success begets success. Something magical happens when it feels as if all the stars line up and the power of the universe is on your side. It creates an energy that I believe attracts the interest of others. Such interest can be grounded in good intentions of joining a cause or organization they believe in, but surely some people are motivated by their own selfish interests. Developing the stomach to walk away from even good opportunities because they might take you off course is the key to staying on course.

Fran would say, "The first one who speaks in a negotiation loses." In the context of clarity, a leader loses when he or she chooses anything other than commitment to solving the problems that the organization exists to solve.

You lose with your constituents.
You lose with your employees.
You lose with your donors.
And, ultimately, you lose with those who
will benefit from your work.

I'm not talking about saying no to things that are blatantly obvious. If you make chocolate candy, you probably want to pass on the opportunity to make tires. If you teach Latin, you probably want to pass on the opportunity to teach modern Hebrew. Those decisions are easy. I'm talking about discerning between good things that are close to the fabric of your organization. One may be right while the other only feels right. The latter can be detrimental because it drains resources and burns dollars that might have been used more effectively elsewhere.

In a post-recession era, donor dollars are more important than ever. It is vital that those of us who lead nonprofit organizations are able to provide a clear return on investment for those who choose to invest in us. You might be able to convince someone once to give to your cause or organization, but you'll have to earn that second gift through careful and thoughtful attention to leveraging the power of "no."

The Dashboard Effect

As interest in Soles4Souls grew, so did the need to protect and preserve the clarity that provided the path to where we are today. When we were just beginning to get traction, and personal interviews were becoming more common, I found myself being asked questions I was unprepared to answer. I was quick enough on my feet to know what to say, but inside I was screaming at myself.

I don't mean to suggest that I wasn't involved in the details. The difficulty was that as my travel schedule had become more intense, I was missing more campfire meetings. I grew dependent upon other people to inform me about what was happening in the day-to-day operations. This left me anxious since I had a lot invested, personally and professionally, in making sure this dream became a sustainable reality.

David (executive vice president), Kevin (chief financial officer), and I were talking one afternoon when I shared my frustration. I wanted a dashboard view of Soles4Souls that would give me all the information I needed to stay up to date on the internal operations of the organization. We discussed the items we felt were most important, especially the ones I would most likely be asked about in an interview. Together, we were able to craft a report that listed who would be responsible for certain information, and how the workflow would happen on a regular basis.

Keep in mind that we are a young but rapidly growing $75 million organization. Putting that size and complexity onto a dashboard not only helped inform me and give me confidence that we were heading in the right direction, it also refined our thinking about what we were measuring and provided data to support what we were telling our donors and ourselves about our work and efforts.

Early in my career in the shoe industry, I worked for a nationwide shoe retail chain and was tasked to correct underperforming store locations. Typically, I would assume the role of manager at the identified location for about ninety days. One of the first things I always did was pull employee schedules and match them against actual work habits. I needed to find out who was consistently late, who didn't show up at all, and who took on additional hours. Before I ever met anyone, I could make an educated guess as to who was contributing to the problem and which employees were worth investing in further.

Work schedules weren't the only indicator that I evaluated, but I was convinced that people who were willing to show up consistently and even take on additional shifts were going to be catalysts in my plan to reverse declining store sales. Why? Because they were focused on one goal: to do the work necessary to achieve the agreed-upon end result. If I was going to have any hope at turning the store around, I needed a team that was clear on the objectives and goals and was ready to do the work necessary to keep the retail location alive.

I reflect on what I learned during those retail days each Friday morning as I review each updated dashboard that captures the activity of the current week. Whether I'm on a plane, heading to an interview, or meeting with potential donors, board members, or industry executives, I'm able to quickly see a snapshot of Soles4Souls and the progress throughout the week. It's much easier to keep a complex organization on course when you know where you need to be and are able to compare it to where you are headed.

Clarity is essential. Data doesn't lie. Dashboards deliver the harmony or dissonance of the two while offering the opportunity to adjust if and when necessary.

Wherever You Are ... Be There

Clarity isn't just about mission statements and values, organizational charts and job descriptions, or numbers and reporting mechanisms. Clarity is an exercise in being present. When you are absolutely clear about your goal, singularly focused on protecting and perpetuating the end result of that goal, and stubbornly committed to staying the course in spite of the best intentions and persuasive efforts of others, you are living in the moment and aware of the great need and opportunity that surrounds you.

On a recent trip back from Haiti along with several others who had been providing medical care to people struggling to survive, we immediately began sharing our common observations of the devastation, suffering, and hopelessness that appeared irreversible. It was particularly overwhelming this trip.

One woman in the group we met was trying to process everything she had seen and experienced. I did my best to share a few funny stories and make her laugh. I told her more about Soles4Souls and how we had a plan to provide help and hope to the people of Haiti. She was already familiar with the organization and believed in our work. What she couldn't understand was how we found the strength to continue to return and invest in Haiti when the situation seemed impossible.

I didn't know what to say to comfort her. The only words that came to mind were, "Wherever you are ... be there." What I was trying to tell her was that when you feel overwhelmed by a task or goal, the temptation is to withdraw when the appropriate response is to engage.

The following day, as I took some time for myself before heading back to the office, I reflected on what I had told her. The most important part of life is showing up and being present. "Wherever you are ... be there" means:

Live life to the fullest.
Impact people every day.
Be present in the moment.

Sometimes that leads to pain.
Sometimes that leads to joy.
Sometimes it leads to confusion.
Sometimes it leads to clarity.

One ancient Hebrew writer said it like this, "There is a time for everything under heaven."

Gandhi said, "We must be the change we want to see in the world."

Being present is the ultimate gift we can give others. The challenge is not to live a life avoiding personal investment, even if it's costly. We must involve ourselves in the world during the days and moments of our life; it is the only path to being fully human. A distracted life is an unsatisfied life.

My daughter, Melissa, has heard me say over and over again in her twenty-one years of life that she can do anything she wants to do if she will just apply herself and look for opportunities to share her gifts and abilities with others. I'm always amazed how my decision to share with others—whether that be time, wisdom, or money—never returns empty.

Being there is about creating a new reality, one that is better than the present condition. It might be a renewed commitment to leverage your personal ambition to improve the quality of life for another. It might be a renewed dedication to accomplish more than you first thought possible and to strive to achieve new heights of impact and change.

If we are going to follow Gandhi's wisdom and embody the change we wish to see in the world, we must begin with "Wherever you are . . . be there." If we accept what the ancient Hebrew writer said, then we must recognize that our time is now. The opportunity is constantly before us to be present, invest ourselves in others, and make a measurable difference.

Clarity offers us the strength to dream about specific ways to operate within our core competencies to improve the lives of others, even when it may seem impossible to think one person might be able to accomplish anything. Clarity ensures that we are not caught settling for almost or good intentions.

TWO

Build the community you want, not the one you can afford

"Hire people who are better than you, then leave them
to get on with it . . . Look for people who will aim for
the remarkable, who will not settle for the routine."
—David Ogilvy

"Push money" is used to move under-performing product in
the shoe industry. A salesperson is given extra incentives for
selling a particular pair of shoes. The shoes assigned push
money are usually not performing as well as the top one or
two competing models on the market. Discounting would
devalue the entire brand. Push money, though, preserves the
integrity of the brand and often solves the unit sales crisis.

As someone responsible for getting the order, I paid attention to push money. It offered me the chance to increase my income. I discovered early in my career that I always found a way to move the most shoes that carried the greatest personal incentives. This is an important lesson I carried with me into management and, now, nonprofit work.

I don't trust people who say they aren't motivated by money. That may sound harsh, but the reality is that we all are motivated by money. I think people assume that money is somehow inherently tainted. I don't get that. Money is a tool that allows us to live the life we want or at least can afford. Money gives us the margin to donate and support causes and organizations we believe in. It offers us the means to take vacations, purchase clothes and shoes, invest, and participate in a variety of other activities.

Money is not inherently evil. Money can bring about a lot of very good things, including allowing organizations like Soles4Souls to recruit and retain the best talent on the market to meet the growing demands of those in need.

The Great Controversy

When I entered nonprofit work, I didn't see much that was different from the for-profit environment other than what the organization did with the bottom line. The ultimate goal was not to improve shareholder value but to solve a specific problem. I was blown away by how this philosophy created so much controversy among the entrenched nonprofit establishment and by how much scrutiny it garnered.

Soles4Souls, as much as any other American nonprofit, is absolutely transparent. Every year we hire external auditors to conduct a complete financial review of our operations. We then use that audited information to complete the infamous "Form 990" IRS return—the annual microscopic examination the Federal government requires of every major nonprofit. Transparency is ensured by making these returns available online so the American public can easily scrutinize every detail if so desired. Soles4Souls is no different, and every year we have filed a complete and accurate return.

My commitment to running Soles4Souls as a business, however, coupled with our great success, has subjected us to more than one local journalist in search of a story. Last year, the largest newspaper in town showed up to research Soles4Souls for an investigative feature. Apparently, they thought the amount of money we were generating annually and the amount of money we were investing in our employees meant we were doing something questionable.

With nothing to hide, we invited them in. It certainly wasn't the reception they were expecting. After two weeks, they found nothing that would suggest we were anything but a healthy organization that was growing at a rapid rate and carefully keeping our general and administrative expenses to less than 3 percent of total revenue. I think they left scratching their heads because they had never seen an organization like ours, especially in the nonprofit world.

If they were looking to dig up dirt on us, they failed miserably. In the end, they published a front page story that highlighted our success and disclosed the same information that was already available to the public through our tax returns. We ended up purchasing a series of full-page ads in the same newspaper to promote our work in subsequent editions. For every critic I find, I also hear a tinge of jealousy that need not exist. I'm running Soles4Souls no different than if I were still an executive in the shoe industry striving to improve sales, minimize expenses, and invest for the long-term sustainability by hiring the best and paying competitive salaries.

The unconventional Approach

My personal opinion is that money is not the root of the great controversy about what nonprofits should or should not pay their employees. The objection is grounded in the false assumption that people who work for nonprofits should assume they are worth less than the person performing similar responsibilities in a for-profit context. Such reasoning is faulty at best.

Much of the stigma associated with nonprofit workers' salaries can be tied back to early American colonial life when it was necessary for the wealthy to feel validated as human beings by helping people who seemingly couldn't help themselves. It was essential for them not to eradicate this group but perpetuate their existence. The wealthy needed the poor perhaps as much as the poor needed the wealthy.

That's absolutely crazy!

The goal of nonprofits should be to solve problems and eliminate the source of the injustice completely. I hope one day Soles4Souls goes out of business because we've done our job so well that everyone on this planet has shoes. I'm not fearful of that happening—I'm striving for it.

The primary way in which I address the problems I have set out to solve is through the people on my team. People are the most expensive part of any implementation effort. Once the strategy has been set, it's vital that the leader support and invest in that plan by hiring the right people. An unwillingness to invest heavily in people sets your organization or cause up for failure from the beginning.

Hire the Best, Pay the Best

To the leader who argues that nonprofits shouldn't compete with for-profit–level salaries to attract the best employees, I would argue that today is a new day. The world has changed and continues to change. It's evolving, so we must surround ourselves with experts if we want to do our work with excellence. There is absolutely no way for any one person to keep up with all the ins and outs of things like communication strategy, technology platforms, and donor engagement. Therefore, the leader has to surround him- or herself with the right people who will hold the leader up and take the organization to the next level.

To the nonprofit leader who believes its donors will be furious to discover a charitable organization paying employees competitive wages, I would argue such reasoning merely projects the leader's personal preferences and inhibitions rather than the heart of the donors, the organization, or the cause. How do I know this is true? Because my donors are not upset at me for paying my employees appropriately for their expertise.

I'm growing weary of the long-winded, ill-informed conversations about what donors care about and what they don't. Donors are not upset and outraged by how much people are paid. Donors want impact, results, and the opportunity to make a larger footprint through your cause or organization.

What donors react to negatively is when the lines of expense and impact have been crossed and the net result is more expense than impact.

As a philanthropist myself, I'm very skeptical of any cause or organization that is not development driven. I know it takes money to accomplish just about anything. I'm not referring to the negative expression of this such as manipulation or illegitimate attempts to control people and circumstances. I know that it costs money to hire people, develop programs, sustain efforts, and create a long-term impact. Therefore, any nonprofit organization that doesn't recognize this and act upon it must not be interested in solving problems.

> I hope one day Soles4Souls goes out of business because we've done our job so well that everyone on this planet has shoes.

Our culture does not need more commentators and consultants. I'm not interested in funding more people to evaluate, plan, and recommend changes. I am inspired by people who have done things that didn't make sense, shouldn't have worked, and reversed established precedent.

People Aren't Overhead

Mrs. Busch could have seen me as just another student, but she didn't. I could view my employees as overhead, but I don't. I believe the very reason we have little turnover and have been able to assemble a highly functional group of subject-matter experts is because embedded into our philosophy is the belief that everyone is at the table because they bring something of value. To that end, they are expected to bring that value every day.

We don't just pay people competitively because it makes us feel better about ourselves. That would be no different from the worldview that we are trying to refute. The people who are part of Soles4Souls are expected to perform at their best consistently. It's important for the executive management to catch people doing the right things and look for ways to reinforce that behavior.

People are leaders. I don't hire workers, because they cost me money. Workers wait to be told what to do, when to do it, and they want someone else to approve of their work. Leaders assess, act, evaluate, and do it all over again. This means it's the responsibility of the executive management of Soles4Souls to create a culture of empowerment.

When I was the senior executive of a shoe company, I had salespeople who made more than I did. It never bothered me, because I remembered how hard it was to get the order and how motivated I was when I was given incentives to perform at certain levels. I never placed limits on what my salespeople could earn. This garnered a great deal of criticism from my peers who seemed bothered by the idea that someone else might earn more than they did in a given year. What those people could never wrap their mind around was the fact that we needed the sales people to sell in order to make the rest of the company function.

The primary question at Soles4Souls is, How can we get more shoes on people's feet? It's not how much revenue we can achieve, as if that was an end in of itself. Rather, it is about expanding our capacity to help more people, give away more shoes, and move closer to achieving our goal of giving a pair of shoes to every man, woman, and child in need. If more revenue means we can give away more shoes, why wouldn't I want to invest in the people necessary to keep pushing this model to the limits? And why would any donor ever complain about increased effectiveness and impact?

It's Not All Business

I don't want to leave you with the impression that working at Soles4Souls is just about the business at hand. Because we depend on one another to bring our best to the table each and every day, there is an emotional connection that fosters a sense of connectedness and family. The fallacy that non-profit workers shouldn't be paid for the value they bring to the table leads organizations to hire people who will perform at differing degrees of intensity. If everyone is paid the same and the pay is already low, this creates frustration on behalf of those who are engaged and achieving results. There is little chance a collaborative environment will become anything other than the regular pep talk at staff meetings.

This is not the case at Soles4Souls. We recognize that those who remain at the organization are valued participants in the journey to give away one pair of shoes every second. This sense of equality can be seen in my open-door policy where anyone, even donors, can come directly to my office and interact with me. In fact, our entire executive management follows this policy. It's vital that we not create barriers to conversation but empower the experts we retain to perform at their highest levels.

We also have a lot of fun with each other. Kevin, our chief financial officer, is the oldest employee. Each month we have a birthday party for him. It's crazy, makes no sense, and isn't necessary. Why do we do it? Because it's fun. We are peers. That means we work together, and we play together. We go to battle together, and we celebrate together.

The Pareto Principle Spells Failure

There is a principle you learn in business school applied to almost every facet of life. It's called the Pareto Principle: 20 percent of the people do 80 percent of the work. If only a few people in a nonprofit are paid well and the rest are paid at a minimum, then the Pareto Principle will be true. At Soles4Souls, we hire the best and pay the best because I want 100 percent of the people doing the 100 percent of the work that is within their area of expertise. An unexpected benefit is when everyone on the team knows that everyone is bringing his or her best to the table, team members are viewed as peers rather than subordinates.

It is very difficult to create the common trust necessary to function as a team when only a few people are paid to carry the burden of the workload. My employees need to know that I am behind them. They also need to know that they are not the only ones working as hard as they are.

I'm one of the first ones in the building each morning and often the last one to leave. I make myself available as technology allows. I want my team to know that while I expect a lot from them, they should expect the same or, perhaps, an even greater level of effort from me. When I become a taskmaster issuing edicts from above, I perpetuate the Pareto Principle and erode the collective energy needed to keep the team moving forward together.

More than Giving Shoes Away

I don't want to leave you with the impression that the people who we hire are above adversity. They are regular people who bring a great deal of passion and expertise to the table. This means they experience life at its best and at its worst.

We hired one employee who previously owned and operated a small but profitable catering service. Business was strong until the recession hit. As people cut back on the extras in life, her business was impacted. For the first time in her life, she wasn't sure what direction her life was headed. She desperately wanted a new beginning but had no idea where she might be able to find one.

The situation didn't get any better. As money became tight and then completely ran out, she was evicted from her apartment and forced to live in her car. She found herself in a situation she didn't deserve and she was uncertain about the prospects of anything reversing the compounding, complex tension of being homeless.

She continued to apply for jobs and look for work. She worked when she could, but it was still not enough to move into another apartment and reestablish a physical address she could call home. Many nights were spent crying herself to sleep wishing and praying for a better day to come sooner rather than later.

I can't imagine what it must have been like for this proud, self-sustaining woman to find herself in such a terrible cocktail of circumstances. She eventually found her way to Soles4Souls, not looking for a hand out but a hand up. She presented herself well, never mentioning her situation, and was chosen to fill the open position.

I wasn't involved in the hiring process because I was out of the office traveling for a couple of weeks when all this took place. As soon as I arrived back in the office, I went over and gave her a big hug. She is about five feet tall, and I'm six feet four inches tall, so I think she was a little overwhelmed.

I paid attention to her work, which seemed to be conducted with an intensity almost unparalleled by anyone else in the office. She was quiet, did excellent work, and performed with a high level of accuracy. This is the description of a model employee, not a woman wondering what the weather will be like so she knows how many blankets she'll need to keep warm.

Somehow, though, I got the feeling that something wasn't right. I couldn't put my finger on it, but I knew it was fairly intense. I asked her direct manager if he knew anything. That's when we both learned the extent of the situation. My heart sank. I didn't need to travel around the world to find someone who needed hope . . . she was on my payroll!

I called her into my office one morning soon after my discovery. We discussed the situation, both shedding a few tears in the process, and then I walked over to my desk and pulled out a set of keys and gave it to her. She looked confused. I told her that these were the keys to a condo I owned in town. She was free to stay there as long as she liked, under the condition that no rent would be charged until she was well back on her feet. I would wait for her to initiate the conversation. She agreed. We hugged.

To this day, she remains a model employee and one of the best tenants I have ever had. I don't tell you this because I want you to think I'm some great hero. I tell you this because I want you to go and do the same. I didn't do anything different for this employee than Mrs. Busch did for me. Just as I was given hope, I gave this employee hope.

Hiring the best people doesn't absolve them from adversity, but it does make me want to ensure there are no obstacles preventing them from becoming the rock stars they were designed to be. I receive a return that is much greater than any risk I take by investing significantly in the people on my team.

It's all about people. The most important decision you can make is to invest as much as you can, even more than you might have ever dreamed, to ensure you have assembled a team that will fight for one another as you weave together your collective efforts and expertise to give hope to others, whether that be through homes for the homeless or shoes for the shoeless. The community you create will determine the impact you will have.

THREE

sustain impact by Engaging others

"You give but little when you give of your possessions.
It is when you give of yourself that you truly give."
—Kahlil Gibran

In the early days, I knew we needed to find an infusion of cash that would keep us alive long enough to get some traction. I was able to secure a grant from a major trade association. That was important seed money to get this new charity moving forward quickly.

We were just beginning, so we knew our reputation was on the line. Under the terms of the grant, we hosted charity-benefit concerts. I hoped that these events would also help us gain recognition and spread the word about Soles4Souls to the masses. Isn't hosting a headline concert with an A-list celebrity musician the ticket every nonprofit dreams about to help build awareness about their cause or organization? Of course! I knew we had stumbled onto our chance to make it big and get there fast.

I feared, internally, that the money spent on the concerts might not produce much more than a good time for some and a hangover for others. I asked myself, How was a concert really going to get someone involved in what we were doing?

Nevertheless, we moved forward with the plan and executed several successful charity-benefit concerts that attracted thousands. Each time I enjoyed the live music and the electric atmosphere. Each time I connected with friends and had a good time, even though I was overseeing all the details of the events.

I also remember standing in the middle of one of the venues just hours after the concert ended, consumed by the sound of silence coming from a place buzzing just hours earlier. I walked through the event site looking at all the trash, empty cups, and ticket stubs scattered everywhere.

I reached in my pocket and pulled out my ticket stub. I wondered how many people had even taken a moment or two to notice the information on the stub itself. How many were really interested in Soles4Souls, and did anyone walk away with an interest in joining our newly founded effort to provide shoes to people in need?

I feared the worst. In an honest attempt to expose a lot of people to the mission and motives of Soles4Souls, we had been lost in the clutter of conversation, alcohol, and the busyness of tomorrow.

Lost in the Details

Soles4Souls was the first charity to organically emerge from within the shoe industry with the intent of distributing shoes. I knew the magnitude of what we had accomplished with just a little effort after the Asian tsunami and the Katrina disaster. This little start-up was capable of accomplishing big things. All we needed was a steady stream of new people catching the vision, spreading the word, and actively participating through donations, contributions, and distributions.

Just as I suspected, the concert we had produced did not make a lasting impression. We had created a lot of noise, but that noise lasted until the last note was sung and the last chord strummed. Then, people went back to their normal lives. I knew it wasn't because Soles4Souls didn't have a compelling vision with a contagious mission and purpose. We had been lost in the details.

The entire purpose of the event was designed around raising awareness for Soles4Souls, the emerging nonprofit jewel in an industry not known for its charitable habits. After spending a lot of money to produce a well-executed, well-attended event, we didn't accomplish much more than having fulfilled our contractual obligations. The haunting question for me was what did Soles4Souls have to show for the nearly $2 million invested in the event? The answer was nothing.

I remain grateful for the initial grant because it was an investment in me and Soles4Souls, an unproven charity at the time. The leaders of this industry-leading organization remain friends to this day. I know there were other options available, but they chose Soles4Souls. Even if we failed to gain an incredible amount of traction or harness the power of awareness during those concerts, this group propelled us forward with a momentum that few experience.

The Problem with Awareness

One thing I learned quickly in the nonprofit world is that all leaders are infatuated with how to build awareness. They believe that if enough people know about an organization or cause, then a certain number of them will gain interest and eventually become fully actualized donors, participants, and evangelists.

I know I'm not the smartest guy in the world. I don't have a bunch of letters that follow my name and all the other stuff that is associated with being an expert, but I do know this: just because people have knowledge of what you are doing, doesn't mean they will take the initiative to become involved. I know that never worked on the sales floor, and I would challenge anyone to show me how that translates into dollars, donors, and evangelists for a particular cause or organization.

My experience with the charity-benefit concerts taught me that awareness is a very expensive endeavor that is as fleeting as the wind. It's impossible to know what direction it is headed, how to capture it, and when its force will fill your sails and carry you forward. I resolved then that awareness shouldn't be the objective.

As we've become more successful as a charity, I am presented with more opportunities to build awareness for Soles4Souls. Each and every time I tell them what I learned long ago: engagement is of greater value than awareness. I'd rather spend money to get people involved in a shoe distribution than to gather thousands for an event that might capture the attention of one or two well-meaning, good-hearted people who believe in what we are doing but are largely uninterested in joining us in our work.

As a retail salesperson and as a corporate executive, I was not measured or compensated based upon the number of people who were aware of our new product, in-store sales and promotions, or geographic location. My job was to get them in the store to buy shoes. If they came to the store, they were going to leave with a pair of shoes. Similarly, nonprofit organizations must demand that they "make a sale" by getting people to fully invest in their cause.

The Potential of Engagement

We have to constantly remind ourselves that just because people know the "who" and the "what" of our organization, that doesn't mean they will instantly become donors, activists, or evangelists for our cause.

We continue to receive countless opportunities to host headline events designed to raise awareness for Soles4Souls. I usually decline because I know it's probably going to cost me a lot of money with little to show for it in the end. Before pursuing greater attention to your organization or cause, keep in mind what awareness does not do:

Awareness doesn't generate contributions.
Awareness doesn't inspire social change.
Awareness doesn't motivate people to action.

Instead of awareness, I look for engagement. I want people to do more than interact with our work at Soles4Souls from a distance. I want people to know that we do more than sponsor special events or concerts. At the end of the day, Soles4Souls gains very little from achieving awareness. Where we see the greatest results is when people participate in our service trips, host shoe drives, and purchase from businesses we've partnered with in the footwear industry.

Awareness creates more spectators, and spectators rarely get in the game or even stay plugged in for very long. Engagement represents a sense of ownership and commitment on behalf of an individual that becomes the fabric of a lasting relationship and long-term results.

The Excitement of Impact

There is something exciting that happens when people get involved in what you are doing. One new way people can choose to get involved with Soles4Souls is by traveling with us to conduct shoe distributions. It's more than providing an adventure travel option. These are people who are giving up their time and money to experience what our organization does for people in need.

I knew this would become a popular option. What I didn't expect was how fast the trips would fill and the speed at which we would have to add new trips. Most nonprofits stop short of asking people to get involved in the work they are doing. The prevailing nonprofit model for much of the twentieth century was the donor funds the work someone else does. There was a time when this model worked very well. Corporations would lean heavily on employees to participate so they could report the level of employee participation in corporate charitable goals.

The primary emphasis was for individuals to outsource relief efforts to someone else. That model is rapidly changing. Many people are no longer interested in outsourcing relief but being intimately involved. They welcome the opportunity to join the frontline efforts of organizations and causes they believe in and support. Don't look at them as simply donors—they want to be partners.

This new interest in personal involvement has created a level of excitement that creates evangelists who are leveraging their personal networks to influence the share of mind, time, and dollars of those who know, like, and trust them. No amount of corporate employees could create and sustain the same level of energy the new donor brings to organizations that offer them the chance to engage on the front line.

Engagement Demands a Plan

One place where we have continued to make significant investments is Haiti. Even though much of the initial relief efforts have ceased, the cameras have stopped rolling, and these people have been largely forgotten, I have a plan. My plan is about establishing a new economy, not merely funneling more money to people in need. I want to help these people experience the joy of self-sustainment and the hope that comes as a result of it. However, I'm also committed to provide whatever relief I can until the baton can be passed and their new economy is in full swing.

After returning from one of my first week-long trips to Haiti to ensure that our shoe distributions were progressing in the way they should, I was completely overwhelmed, disgusted, and angry at what I found.

It wasn't about the shoes. They were being delivered just fine: safely, securely, and in small enough doses to get on the feet of people who needed them. I was grateful to our many partners on the ground who have helped from the beginning.

But I was extremely angry because I saw total chaos and a complete lack of vision to help the survivors, even as they lay dying of disease and starvation in horrible conditions.

You may have heard of these tent cities. The reality is that these are hodgepodge neighborhoods thrown up hastily and lashed together with tarps, twine, and rope. They are devoid of hope. Very few residents know where their next meal is coming from. Children can't go to school or get clothes or clean water. Parents are weak from starvation because they give any scraps of food to their children. The UN and local government seems to be holding out for a miracle rather than putting any concrete plan in place.

There are even confirmed stories of child predators entering the country and posing as relief workers. When I heard that, I shook my head and said, "No, that's not right. That couldn't be." But I was wrong, and I cried. I've never heard of such pure evil in my life.

The first night we were there, a riot broke out because residents of the Tent "Atrocity" were showing their frustration. Our team was uncomfortable and we certainly didn't understand the real conditions until we spent a few days there, speaking with parents, children, teachers, missionaries, and volunteers. Haiti's real disaster wasn't just on January 12, 2010. It's happening right now and will continue unless a plan for a different, sustainable future is put in place.

It's easy to sit in our favorite chairs in our safe neighborhoods and skim through what we perceive to be saturated coverage of the people of Haiti, but we must not allow ourselves to become numb. Engagement doesn't afford us that option. When we become involved, particularly when we look into the eyes of another hurting human being, it's nearly impossible for us to not do something to help.

I've never seen or smelled anything like what I witnessed in Haiti. I threw up a few times because of the utter despair and horrific stench of the place. I didn't know it was possible to survive in a perpetual state of hell on earth.

My heart breaks each time I think about one of the beautiful children reaching for and holding my hand. They are so incredibly precious, and they don't understand that their country is shattered. They know a real bad thing has happened,

> Haiti's real disaster wasn't just on January 12, 2010. It's happening right now and will continue unless a plan for a different, sustainable future is put in place.

but then their childlike sweetness takes hold and they laugh, run, and skip. And my heart breaks, because they have no future the way things stand right now.

Soles4Souls, I resolved, would not sit by and do nothing. Our only option was to chart out a concrete, sustainable plan of action. We never intended to drop off a million pairs of shoes and say, "Okay, best of luck to y'all." We've always been very careful to be sustainable in every area we choose to invest. That word may get thrown around a lot in the nonprofit world, but we're committed to it.

Haitians need housing. They need jobs. They need education. They need micro-enterprise solutions. They need access to clean water, food, and medical care. Yes, they need shoes and clothing—but most of all, they need hope!

We can't put a giant hope Band-Aid on the country with good intentions. Haitians will step up and make it happen if we help eliminate the barriers standing in their way.

This might mean funding small businesses or creating manufacturing opportunities. It certainly means secure housing, education, and medical care. As we help, Haitians help themselves in ways that will create their own economic benefits. The world will see incredible things happen, and Haitians will be the ones to pay it forward. In this way, we can help change their trajectory. We're not just providing shoes; we're providing a bridge of access to a better life.

There is no concert big enough, no budget deep enough, and no advertising broad enough to match the impact that results from those engaged in improving the lives of people in need by doing something measurable.

I represent the new donor. I'm not interested in outsourcing it to a big, bloated, faceless nonprofit. I'm interested in sharing this passion with those ready to use all their available resources of time, talents, and treasure to take action in Haiti and any other place around the world or at home where there are people hurting and living in fear of never being able to know a life other than the hell that surrounds them today.

Awareness leaves us with the knowledge that people are hurting. Engagement asks "What's the plan?" and "How can I get involved?" Awareness allows us to use our busyness as an escape clause. Engagement refuses to ignore the need.

FOUR

create More Margin to
Do More Mission

"... to have no cash at all means ...
absolute powerlessness."
—Histoire de Ma Vie

Money is an unusual subject in the nonprofit world. It is coveted and confusing at the same time. Every business lives and dies by its ability to fund itself. This is a reality that exists in for-profit businesses and nonprofits. Cash is king. Period.

It seems like the nonprofit world places a close watch on those who are successful. It's as if certain people are convinced that any organization that has an exceptional ability to raise cash is automatically suspect.

There is no other organization other than the church that embodies the extremes of the conversation of funding. There are church leaders who believe that money is a resource to accomplish the mission and vision of a particular conversation, and some who would rather pull their toenails off before talking directly and frankly about money.

It seems strange to think that an organization that lives or dies by its ability to fund its mission and make a difference in the world would be shy when it comes to the conversation of money. In fact, one might think that the nonprofit leader would be unapologetic in his or her pursuit of funding, which increases the capacity to accomplish the mission and make an impact.

Such is not the case. A quiet understanding conveyed by other nonprofit leaders is that because fundraising is necessary, you need to hire development professionals. These hired guns take care of the dirty work so the executive director can focus on more important goals. I don't get that! What's more important than being right in the middle of raising all the money you can raise so you can do more with it?

Money is a peculiar subject, indeed. It presents a paradox some leaders are ill-prepared to deal with rationally and professionally. The posture by far too many leaders is one that reveals who is interested in impact and who is interested in avoiding criticism.

Nonprofits Should Talk More About Money

Money is what allows organizations and causes to create change and make a difference. Personally, I think there is too little talk about money, mission, impact, and change in the nonprofit world. Though there are some good reasons why money isn't talked about, there are great reasons why money should be talked about even more.

Money is measurable. You can't talk yourself out of anything when it comes to dollars and cents. You are what your balance sheet says about you. If your expenses are out of line with your revenue and you're making decisions that are placing the fiscal integrity of your organization at risk, then you should rethink your strategy. If our personal checkbooks provide evidence of what is important, the same must be true about the way we spend the money within the organizations we represent. What we say about ourselves must be consistent with our behavior. Donors will be able to tell the difference. The unforgivable sin is duplicity.

Money marks engagement. Money is an external, measurable indicator that you've truly engaged another person. Another way to say it is that giving is an outward side of an internal, emotional commitment to an organization or cause. An individual's willingness to give money to your cause means he or she has engaged with your messaging and mission in a real, practical way.

> Only in America can the conversation of money flow so freely and the criticism come so quickly while the willingness to share with others around the world happens so inconsistently and infrequently.

Money expands your capacity. The more money you have, the more mission you can accomplish. Nonprofits need to look beyond the "just getting by" strategy and start planning for ways to achieve a funding level that will allow you to thrive. Change the conversation from "What is at risk of being underfunded or not funded at all?" to "Where is our next greatest opportunity to invest?"

Why would I ever shy away from a conversation about money? In fact, I probably should talk more about it since the stakes are so high with Soles4Souls.

Money, Money, Money

Let's be honest. No matter our personal comfort level with the subject of money, it is the tool that allows organizations and causes to exist. Is it possible to be a nonprofit and not be focused on money? Yes. But you will needlessly struggle for every small victory instead of thriving in an effort to make a measurable difference.

Money is a means to an end. If we are leading organizations that are truly about making a change in the world, then why do we fear the very thing that gives us the ability to accomplish the work we have set out to do and share our passion with others?

Soles4Souls has definitely faced some controversy when it comes to money. None of it is warranted. Rather, it is the suspicion of those who have never been responsible for leading organizations and accomplishing larger-than-life goals.

Our story is unique in that we weren't a struggling nonprofit for very long. Through some very critical partnerships formed early on, we have been able to leverage the cash from those relationships to create a forward momentum that is quickly propelling beyond the $100 million mark.

At Soles4Souls, I take the subject of money and the creation of cash as seriously as I did when working in the shoe industry. My job as a major shoe company corporate executive was to ensure revenue was generated to operate the business. I knew we would live or die by our ability to increase sales. There had to be money to fund research and development, new business ventures, marketing, production, payroll, etc. That meant we had to generate a steady stream of revenue. Without cash, we couldn't operate.

Further, I knew that my ability to consistently meet sales goals and raise total revenues year-over-year meant that we could sustain ourselves long enough to earn the respect of the industry and the loyalty of the customer. I translated this drive to the nonprofit world.

If our goal is to give away shoes, the more money we can generate affords us greater opportunity to give away even more shoes. We are then able to scale the organization to a level that can sustain this effort. Without long-term commitments, true change can't happen.

I'm convinced that a deficiency in the area of revenue creation is the primary reason some nonprofits are ineffective. I hear it all the time:

- "You can't expect a nonprofit to manage itself like a for-profit business."
- "People don't have as much to give."
- "We have to run a tight ship, so that means long-term planning is the first to go."
- "If you make too much money, then people will think you're just in it for the money."

I'm most discouraged when I hear how some nonprofit executive directors are not taking paychecks because there isn't enough cash to go around. It's simply not realistic to think that this way of living and operating as an organization is sound, and I still can't accept it as normal.

Maybe you find joy and satisfaction in a life of suffering, trials, and tribulations. If that's what it means to be a nonprofit leader, then I'm out.

cash creates Margin

While money is absolutely vital to organizational stability and health, I want to be clear that money is not the end goal. I focus my efforts on creating cash because cash creates margin. The more margin that I can create, the more mission we can accomplish.

If my goal was simply to create revenue so I could make a lot of money, drive luxury cars, and live the high life, then criticism would be warranted and necessary. Every would-be critic has found no evidence to substantiate their desire to explain away our success. While we certainly have attracted our share of criticism, it has clearly not impacted our ability to continue to grow and expand our capacity to give more shoes to the shoeless.

Nonprofits exist to create change. We are agents of social good. It is our job as organizations and causes to speak for the voiceless, fight for the weak, show mercy to the struggling, and seek justice for rich and poor, black and white, young and old, powerful and powerless.

At Soles4Souls, we provide shoes to the shoeless. Before I can provide shoes, I have to be able to obtain shoes. Before I can obtain shoes, I have to be able to support an organization to accept and distribute shoes. Before I can facilitate such an organization, I have to have people who will join me in this mission together. I can't do any of this without margin.

I know of no other way to give more shoes away than to create more cash to fuel the growth of our efforts. What drives me is not the exercise of generating revenue. I played that game for a long time. It's not difficult when you have the right system in place. What drives me are the three hundred million children in the world who don't have shoes and are suffering and dying as a result of not having protection from diseases that exists among trash and waste littering the streets of so many countries.

Only in America can the conversation of money flow so freely and the criticism come so quickly while the willingness to share with others around the world happens so inconsistently and infrequently. My pursuit of margin is not a selfish exploit of others. My pursuit of margin is grounded in the knowledge that with more I can do more. That's what keeps me motivated.

cash comes with Accountability

The greatest source of criticism from people today stems from a lack of trust in others. We have little hesitation in giving money to those whom we know, like, and trust. It's important to remember that the question in everyone's mind is always this: Are you going to do what you told me you were going to do?

The donor is not asking, Are you going to try, work hard, or hope for the best? Donors are smart enough to know that some nonprofits are better than others at accomplishing exactly what they said they were going to accomplish. You can be sure that when someone gives you money, buys your product, or invests in your idea, they are signing a contract with you that sets expectations for what will happen with what has been given or invested.

I remember when I decided to invest in a shoe specifically designed to provide comfort and support to a specific group of people. There were already others who had invested in this line of shoes and were successful at gaining market share. However, I believed I could create something that would earn us a place in that particular segment of the industry.

I spent money to engineer plans, develop prototypes, source the product to a trusted manufacturer, and even attend trade shows where I proudly presented the product directly to retailers and the general public. I had a tremendous amount of mental energy and money invested in this product.

Even though we did experience some success, it was not what we needed to justify continuing to invest in this new area. Plus, I had pulled some research and development money from other places to make this new line of shoes successful. So I had to swallow hard, pause momentarily, and make the tough call at shutting down our effort to expand with this new product line. It was difficult to do, but it was the right thing to do.

When donors give nonprofits cash, they expect results. Leaders must understand that when a program, idea, or investment is no longer offering a positive return, then it's time to consider shutting it down. Not doing so harms the relationship with the donor and is wasteful with what we have been given.

Too Many Nonprofits

I have often wondered if there are too many nonprofits in our world. I know this is an unpopular stance to take, and I'm prepared for the criticism to come from the greater nonprofit community. If the social enterprise wing of our economy was operated like a large conglomerate, then site closures, mergers, and acquisitions would occur regularly.

Even if we are able to create more cash than we ever could have imagined, we must recognize that cash is a limited asset. We must do all that we can with what we have been given to ensure the intent of the donor is protected and the object of our work is beneficial.

I'm convinced that we would do better to merge nonprofits with similar goals, mission, and service to create a more powerful, better funded force.

If the end game is to eliminate suffering and elevate the overlooked, then it makes little difference how we are organized if, in fact, we are organized to make a measurable difference and impact. I'm convinced that we could do even greater things if we stopped competing with one another and began working together to fight the world's problems.

Why do we need so many nonprofits focused on the same goal or objective? It's confusing to the donor and creates an unnecessary amount of stress during the giving process. Further, it splits the dollar as nonprofits seek to separate themselves from the pack. The one who really loses in the end is the person everyone says they are fighting for in the first place. The nonprofit that has the greatest chance of achieving the funding levels needed to create a sustainable, long-term impact will take a completely different approach.

Our Donors Deserve an "Apple" Experience

I have to say that I've lived in the PC world my entire professional life. I've never had much interest in Apple or its products. My personal opinion was that it was more for creative types, like writers, designers, etc. Like most businesspeople, all I had known was Windows-based computing.

Everything changed when the iPad was introduced. I was curious about all the things I could do with this revolutionary device. I wanted to try one to see if the iPad was more hype than substance. Would I really be able to work using this device, or is it strictly an entertainment novelty?

I have to say I love my iPad! I take it with me on every trip. Since TSA says it doesn't qualify as a computer, I don't even have to take it out of my bag at security checkpoints. I can read a book, check my e-mail, participate in social media, and do a whole host of other things. I'm becoming more familiar with the business productivity tools, too.

On a recent trip, I realized I had forgotten my power cord. As I approached the Apple Store, I began to wonder if I would feel out of place. When I opened the door and entered the store, I observed a web of activity that was no less than brilliant.

Seconds after entering the store, I was greeted by a friendly individual whose entire goal was to ensure I had the best experience of my life. He asked what I needed, he walked me over to find the cord I needed, escorted me to the desk, charged it to my Apple account on file, said I would receive an e-mail receipt in the next twenty-four hours, and wished me a great rest of my trip.

There was no "you're interrupting my day" attitude, he didn't just point me in the right direction, he didn't make me wait in a long line, he didn't ask me to give a form of payment, he didn't clutter my pockets with another receipt, he didn't try to sell me something else, and he didn't even scold me for using my BlackBerry to check an urgent message during checkout. I was the most important person to him, and he was committed to making sure I didn't have anything but an exceptional experience.

This guy was Apple to me during my time in the store. If Apple as a whole is treating its customers this way, then I completely understand why so many are so loyal to just about anything this organization produces and brings to market.

It occurred to me later that evening that donors should have a similar experience when they interact with Soles4Souls. They are the most important piece to the puzzle of putting shoes on the feet of the shoeless. Without donors we couldn't operate at the same level of impact we have right now. We should do everything in our power to ensure their experience with Soles4Souls is nothing less than exceptional.

This is why I pick up the phone when it rings. This is why I spend time rubbing shoulders with the people who share my passion for giving away shoes rather than lock myself in the executive suite. This is why my staff never transfers anyone to voice mail. Instead, they take a personal message.

The people who fund us aren't interruptions or personal ATMs; they are special people who deserve a consistent, special experience every time they interact with our organization.

I want every person who interacts with Soles4Souls to have an "Apple" experience. Our funding level depends upon it.

Money Forces Tough Decisions

Early on in the life of Soles4Souls, we thought about buying a fleet of trucks. We all did our due diligence to be sure we knew what kind to buy, what was a fair market purchase price, how would we staff drivers, and determined how we would modify our distribution strategy in light of this new option.

We had complete signoff from our board of directors, and everyone on the team agreed this was the right thing to do. The cash was available, and the dealership was ready to broker the deal we had carefully negotiated.

The night before we were supposed to sign the papers, I couldn't sleep. I had this sense that the decision to buy this fleet of trucks was not the best decision we could make. We weren't doing anything wrong. We weren't borrowing money to pay for the vehicles. The plan was in place to hire and manage drivers as well as establish distribution routes, times, etc. Still, something didn't seem right.

Emotionally, we wanted to follow through on our carefully laid out plans when I remembered some great advice I received from a friend: never make a big deal without first sleeping on it. The only problem was now I wasn't sleeping at all. I took it as a sign and called the deal off the next day.

Looking back, it would have been the wrong decision but for all the right reasons. Money forces clarity and pushes individuals and organizations to make a decision. Rarely are those decisions easy. Every person must decide how they will use the excess or margin in their lives. We only get one shot in this life to make a difference in the life of someone else.

The decision rarely is between buying a fleet of trucks or continuing to outsource that function. The decision is more like scaling back in a few areas in order to be able fund organizations that have proven themselves worthy of your donations.

How we spend our money is the best indicator we have of the legacy we will leave behind. This is true for individuals and organizations. What does your posture toward money say about the legacy you're building?

FIVE

Make Decisions That Take You where You want to Go

"How we spend our days is, of course, how we spend our lives."
—Annie Dillard

Making a decision is just as important as making the right decision. There is a lot of weight in a statement like that. What is the right decision? How can you know for sure? You can't. It would be great to have some unexplainable insight that would allow you to look into the future to see if a particular decision would prosper or fail miserably. But that only happens in the movies.

Life is a series of decisions, and the decisions that we make take us where we want to go. I'm not suggesting we try to avoid or eliminate the serendipitous events in our life.

When something happens that we haven't planned for or can't explain, we often classify this as tragic.

It's been more than two decades since my brother was killed in a traffic accident. No one could have seen that coming. Timmy was a great man who loved life and his family. He was young but had already used his life to impact others. I made a decision upon his death to carry out his legacy and find a way to do some good while I still had time to spend and life to live.

He didn't decide to die that day any more than the person who caused the accident intended to take his life. It just happened. We must accept that which we can't control and change what we can, realizing that we have but one life to live, and one opportunity to change a life through something as simple as a kind word or gesture.

Why is it that tragic moments bring the most clarity to any given situation? Is it really necessary for us to face our own mortality vicariously through those who've gone before us? The strange paradox of life is, when we finally accept that we are not invincible and won't live forever, that is when we are free to live the life intended for us—one guided by love and the opportunity to give freely.

After 9/11, the American spirit paused for a moment to cry with the hurting, pray with strangers, hold the hands of the newly orphaned children, and wait with hope and great anticipation as the rubble was removed piece by piece. Time seemed to stand still as people questioned life's significance and adjusted their priorities to reflect that newfound sense of self, meaning, and purpose. For a brief moment, life mattered very little beyond the family and friends we love.

We don't have to wait for the next personal or national tragedy, though, before deciding to live with clarity and making decisions that take us where we want to go. The great news is that this can happen today.

Buffalo Wings and Hot Sauce

A friend and I convinced ourselves that we loved buffalo wings and hot sauce enough that we were going to invest in a local franchise of a national chain. We were both very successful in the shoe industry and making great money. We saw this as a chance to not only make a little money but also have a little fun at the same time.

We found the perfect location and talked to a real estate agent who had negotiated a great deal on our behalf. We knew our market plan, launch timeline, and had completed conversations with the chain. The opportunity was ours for the taking. But then I slept on it.

As I mentioned in the previous chapter, this is a key element to any good business decision. The great mistakes I've made in business have been as a result of not taking this advice. Everyone—no matter how rational he or she is—makes decisions emotionally. I'm certainly not anti-emotion, but I do realize that no business transaction should be based solely on emotion. We agreed to reschedule the signing date to give us some time to think it over.

We went to what we had joked would soon be the second best buffalo wings restaurant in town and ordered a few dozen. As we talked, we came to the conclusion that neither one of us knew anything about the restaurant industry. We had great intentions and plenty of extra cash to put into this. If it failed, it would hurt but not bankrupt us.

The next morning I made the phone calls to our real estate agent and the national chain contact, neither of whom was happy to hear our final decision. Each time I think about the choice we made, I am more convinced that it would have absolutely been the wrong investment to make.

> **An architect always learns the function of the space before he or she determines the form of the space.**

Business is business, and this one most likely would have been a successful venture because my friend and I love a good challenge and have always found a way to make something work. We realized, though, that the learning curve was going to be huge and that it would take far more money and time than we were willing to spend figuring out the restaurant business.

Seeing Life Through the Decisions We Make

My greatest fear for Soles4Souls has nothing to do with fiscal integrity or organizational management. Those pale in comparison to what I consider my greatest enemy: time. We cannot take (or waste) too much time in our work. This creates a fast-paced environment at Soles4Souls where team members are expected to react quickly and with great intention. Time is of the essence in everything we do.

One member of my executive team previously worked at another company in a similar position for nearly twenty years. He had a team of people who supported his work and was very comfortable in the way he conducted business. When you work for one organization for that long, you become the organization and the organization becomes you. It's difficult to think of new things and in new ways since there is nothing pushing you to do so. His decision making was slow because he feared making the wrong decision.

He comfortably avoided risk through exhaustive risk assessment analysis, complicated webs of meetings, and endless conversation. This usually resulted in him saying no to anything that stretched him beyond his comfort level. The risk couldn't be greater than what he determined to be a good investment of time, energy, and money.

His first year at Soles4Souls was a difficult transition. He had a much smaller staff, was responsible for more things, and had to live with me incessantly pushing the limits at every turn. I'm convinced he lived scared to death most of the time. After multiple conversations and successes, I had to convince him that it was less important to avoid mistakes than it was to take advantage of every opportunity to make an impact. Decisions would sometimes result in success and sometimes result in failure. As long as we understood why, he was not going to be in trouble or risk losing his job.

The pace of Soles4Souls is swift. None of my team members ever has time to mull things over. As quick as we discover a problem, we create a solution and plan of action. That environment works for some people, but it has been too intense for some to handle. I'm not a taskmaster constantly asking for more and more, but I am driven by the realization that the faster and more efficient we become at distributing shoes, the sooner more people in need will receive them.

Every decision we make either helps us achieve our goal of distributing one pair of shoes every second or distracts and delays us from tackling the challenge at hand. The longer it takes us to accomplish our goal of giving away shoes, the more people who lose their lives as a result of needless exposure to disease and viruses contracted as a direct result of not having shoes.

My commitment to Pakistan is shoes, not politics

Sometimes my decisions are not popular. I've lived long enough to become comfortable with other people, even powerful people, disagreeing with me. I don't make decisions to impress others nor to avoid their criticism. My focus is on helping others and making a difference. As long as I keep that my main goal, then I know I will make decisions that will take me where I want to go.

When I realized the devastation caused by the flooding in Pakistan during the summer of 2010, I was reminded of the day I saw that shoe wash up on the beach during the Asian tsunami. Just as I had felt back then, I knew in this moment that I had to do something to help. It is with that same passion and desire I made a pledge to Pakistan.

The relief workers need shoes.
The survivors need shoes.
The children need shoes.

What I didn't expect was the hate mail I would receive as a result of this decision. To me, this was about helping people in need. To some, this was a move that came with political consequences. That frustrated me. Politics should never be valued more than people. I don't care who you are, where you are from, or what you have done. My commitment is to helping others. I'll leave the politics to the professionals. My heart is saddened when I think about how some have lost sight of the common humanity we share, despite our geographic location or form of government that has authority over us.

Shoes will protect their feet from disease and harm while at the same time give them the confidence to continue pressing forward even though the impact of the floods is nothing short of tragic. A pair of decent shoes is absolutely necessary in order to participate effectively in rescue and rebuilding efforts among broken glass, twisted metal, and raw sewage.

What we have learned and continue to learn through our relief efforts in Haiti is informing our work in Pakistan. My commitment to Pakistan was initially one hundred thousand pairs of shoes, not politics. My prayer is for shoes to become a tangible sign that hope still exists. The decision to help others is the best decision I could have made, even if it costs me a few points in the minds of a segment of the general public.

What They Don't Teach You in School

I never graduated from college. Most people don't know that, and many are surprised when I tell them. They can't seem to reconcile how someone with a high school diploma could ever achieve all that I have. It's as if a piece of paper one receives from an institution after spending six figures and four years guarantees you success.

This is what doesn't add up for me about formal education. A person's ability to complete a set amount of coursework, learn to take tests, and follow the rules never teaches him how to break the system, question authority, or blaze a new trail. The emphasis on fitting into the culture is what is pounded into the minds of too many impressionable young people. It ends up bridling the passion of a world changer and turning him or her into something they never wanted to become.

That being said, I'm not anti-education. I am a product of a series of good decisions and a little bit of luck. I didn't give my daughter an option. She was going to college. I wanted to give her every opportunity to succeed, and I'm confident she is going to do big things. I'm so proud of her commitment to excellence and integrity.

I've also tried to drill into her mind that while college is helpful in developing key disciplines and skills such as critical thinking, the real world is a far different place. What separates those who make it from those who don't is not the ability to read a course syllabus, learn a professor's preferences, and write research papers. It is the decisions you make and your willingness to take risks in hopes of gaining an even bigger reward.

Decisions Lead to Action

Decisions force you to draw boundaries and declare what is most important to you. Decisions call you to action. It's impossible to make a decision without saying yes to one thing and no to another.

I meet a lot of would-be activists looking to change the world who, upon closer look, are much better at enraging a crowd than making change. The real world demands action and results. It achieves nothing to stir emotions if you don't ask people to do something.

I'm always overwhelmed by the stories of nonprofit leaders who feel as if their hands are tied. They want to do something wonderful, but someone told them no. I sympathize with them. No one knows the opportunity or possibility of organizations better than the executive director. It has to be incredibly defeating to know the right thing to do but have your hands tied. My advice is either find a way to untie your hands or find a new organization to lead. It really is that simple.

It's important to know where we are headed. An architect always learns the function of the space before he or she determines the form of the space. Knowing where we are headed becomes a key evaluation marker to ensure we are pushing ourselves in the right direction. When you're not sure about what's ahead, look for the aha moments. When they come, pay attention to them. One aha moment leads to another aha moment. Connect the dots to see the direction you are headed.

Whether you're a single mother, retired professional, young child, or a rising executive, every day presents us with opportunities to make a decision to make a difference in the life of another person. It could be a smile, a handshake, a pat on the back, or any other simple act of kindness. It could be as radical as selling your house, changing jobs, or moving around the world to ensure the needs of others are met in specific and measurable ways.

We must decide what kind of life it is we want to live—and then we need to live it! As we reflect upon what we have become and all we have, it is a reflection of the decisions we have made. What do your decisions say about you? We each are given opportunities to make a difference, so what will be your decision? In the end, almost will never be good enough.

get off the couch

"The way to get started is to quit talking
and begin doing."
—Walt Disney

This particular morning was no different from countless other mornings. I got up, ate a quick breakfast, and headed out the door to the office. My well-maintained and relatively new car started as smooth as ever. I put the car in reverse, pulled out on the street, and started down the path I had driven many times. It was one of those days when you felt like you were ready to conquer the world.

When I finally made it to the interstate, something didn't seem right. I soon realized smoke was coming from my seat. I carefully crossed multiple lanes of traffic to get over to the shoulder with as little fanfare as possible. By the time I had pulled over, the smoke was making it difficult for me to see and breathe. I did my best to unlock the car door, but I couldn't seem to override the power lock system. The windows didn't want to roll down either.

As the smoke filled the car, I wondered how I was going to be able to get out of this situation. After a few seconds, my thoughts changed to how I was going to stay alive. I knew the longer I was in the car with an increased amount of carbon monoxide pouring into the cabin, the more serious the situation became. Thankfully, I was able to get out.

When help arrived, their first concern was assessing how much carbon monoxide I had actually inhaled. I knew it was enough to be considered dangerous. They rushed me to the hospital where the doctor determined I had been poisoned from exposure to the lethal gas. I knew I was lucky to be alive. It's strange how sudden interruptions seem to bring a great deal of clarity to your life.

While waiting to be discharged, I began to think about my daughter, who was sixteen at the time. I wondered what she would say about her dad if I had died as a result of this event. Would she remember me as a corporate executive who had worked hard to achieve success? Would she think of me in terms of the amount of money I had accumulated or the value of things I owned? Or would she say that I loved her and loved life? Would she say that I inspired her to make a difference in the lives of others because that's the example she saw in me?

Turning Forty

Something strange happens when you reach forty years of age. You begin to see life differently. Your twenties are about grabbing life by the throat in hopes of wrestling the world to victory. Your thirties are about getting traction in life. It's the first time in life when people recognize you as a professional, you begin to earn enough to move beyond survival, and you become comfortable in your own skin. There is a lot of momentum that comes from your thirties as you move into your forties. The most unexpected part of turning forty is the built-in introspection that overwhelmingly causes you to think differently about things like family, life, career, and money. It is during this time when your life perspective seems to change.

Some consider your forties middle age. I suppose I might have thought that earlier in life. Now it seems like an incredible moment of opportunity. I have the time, ability, and resources to make a difference. I still had one more step to make: put it all into action.

This is where so many miss the opportunity. The time in which we are alive is very short. I am guilty of thinking I am invincible, that somehow I'm good enough, strong enough, and powerful enough to postpone the end of life until I'm ready. Any sense of control is an illusion and should be carefully evaluated. We only have one life to live, to give, and to offer as a blessing to others. Largely, my life up until this point had been about me, but it didn't need to continue to be that way.

In the days after my roadside episode, I thought a lot about Mrs. Busch and what she had meant to me. I remembered vividly how her kind words of affirmation kept me from ending my life at the time and gave me permission to explore, follow my passion, and create the life I wanted instead of being bound to the one that I was handed. Mrs. Busch gave me what she could, and now I felt like it was time for me to give what I could to others and pay it forward.

Relaxing on the couch

It wasn't but a few weeks later when the Asian tsunami devastated people who had nothing to begin with. When that single shoe washed up on shore, I had a moment of clarity. The burning car, Mrs. Busch, and the hospital all flashed through my mind at once. I knew I had to do something to help.

I couldn't articulate Soles4Souls at the time. I had no concept of an international relief organization, but I was very familiar with the shoe industry. That's when I decided that sitting comfortably on the couch was not an option when I had the contacts, the influence, and the opportunity to do something that mattered. It didn't matter to me that they spoke a different language, had a different skin tone, or worshipped differently than I did. They were human beings who needed help.

I sat up on the couch and reached for the phone. Who was I to sit so comfortably when so many others were emerged in a living hell? The problem with America is not capitalism, but people who are not willing to see the margin in their lives as the chance to make a difference in the life of another. America was built upon a common ethic and commitment to community. When we lose that and build our lives with ourselves at the center, we will decay as fast as we became the world's greatest nation.

The Loss of a Friend

Life has a way of getting your attention whether you want to pay attention or not. Many people believe in the old saying that things happen in threes. I had my experience in the car, the moment of clarity on the couch, so I was waiting to discover what would be the final link in this chain of events.

Soon after the tsunami, a very close business friend dropped dead unexpectedly. There was no warning or explanation. He was a very wealthy man who had been incredibly successful in life. The question that immediately popped into my mind startled me: "What does rich mean?"

We spend our lives striving for something more. We desire nicer cars, bigger homes, and more toys. Professionally, we want recognition by our peers, positions of authority, and a track record that many just dream about. It never occurred to me that I might do something other than live for more of just about everything.

Rich means having the time, money, and freedom to live the life that you want. When most people think about being rich, they dream about the absence of worry, the ability to do or have anything, and the chance to be perceived as important. While some aspect of each of those things exist for the affluent, there is much common ground between the wealthy and the wanting.

Rich people worry. Rich people get frustrated. Rich people struggle finding satisfaction, fulfillment, and meaning too. So questioning the meaning of rich turned my world on its side. I found myself questioning the path I was on. It was a deeply spiritual time in my life. The paradox is this: I have never been so clear about living than in the face of death.

Reclaim Your Life

I chose to leave my corporate career and make Soles4Souls my life's work. Just because I made that decision doesn't mean that is the only option you have available. Maybe you're in your twenties, thirties, fifties, or whatever age and wondering what can you do. You might be discouraged that you can't leave your job and start a nonprofit organization to solve a looming social problem. Maybe you feel backed into a corner with your career and family obligations and think there is no way you can get a do-over in life.

If you're in your twenties, let me encourage you to learn as much as you can about yourself. Surround yourself with people who are better than you at just about anything. Listen, watch, observe, and practice. Change jobs more frequently if you need. Not everyone wakes up one day and recognizes what he or she will do the rest of their life. With the pace at which technology is changing the world, chances are whatever you are doing today won't exist by the end of your career. Even better are the chances of you stumbling into a career that didn't exist when you graduated from college. Use this time to discover who you are, your unique talents, and how you can leverage those skills to help yourself and others.

If you're in your thirties, keep a balance between work and family. Don't be so consumed with building your career that you leave your family behind. Your family will be there when your job fails you and when the company you have been so loyal to decides they no longer need your services. There is no amount of money that will buy you the security you can find in the loving arms of the ones you love and who love you.

If you're in your fifties or older, it's not too late. You may be entering a transitional period in your life that is very similar to those who are in their twenties. Perhaps you are on the brink of retirement. Your identity is wrapped up in your work, your airline rewards account, and your membership to the corporate gym. Retirement does not mark the end of your life but an opportunity to invest in other areas.

The decision I made that day to get off the couch is the same decision we must make every day. I still make that decision daily, even though I'm leading Soles4Souls. We must constantly redirect our life course to ensure we are using the time, gifts, and margin we have to help others in need. To have enough to give something to others is what it really means to be rich. Never be too old to listen, learn, and change. This is the secret to reclaiming your life from the ordinary so that you might be positioned for the extraordinary.

Meet Mr. Important

Airports are a necessary part of modern life. Not everyone has the luxury John Madden has to travel exclusively on the road, even as he did during all his years as an NFL color commentator. We just don't have that kind of time. Many of us are dependent upon airplanes to travel hundreds of miles in a matter of a few hours instead of an entire day. Anyone who has traveled with any regularity knows to expect delays and interruptions. They are a normal part of life. The best thing to do is have your BlackBerry, iPad, laptop, or other device close by with a set of headphones to help pass the time and be as productive as possible.

It amazes me that in every group there is always one person who believes he or she is the most important person in the world. It is his or her world, and we are just lucky to be living in it. There was this one guy who appeared very upset because of a delayed flight. He walked up to the counter, and

I watched closely. I knew something interesting was about to take place, and I had a front row seat. After asking the airline representative a few questions, his face became as red as a tomato. He went from talking to yelling as he said, "Do you know who I am?"

Anyone who knows me knows that I never miss an opportunity to defend someone. This representative handled herself with dignity while this guy just went off on her. So I seized the moment to walk my six-foot, four-inch self over to the counter. I interrupted the conversation and asked the representative for the microphone. She was so flustered she just pointed to it. I leaned over and said calmly, "Excuse me. Does anyone know who this man is? He isn't sure, and we are trying to help him figure it out."

While others thought it was amusing, this guy didn't think it was cute or original. He proceeded to call me every name in the book. I thought I had heard just about everything, but I was impressed with his ability to create a few new ones. He eventually walked away leaving what had become a very uncomfortable and awkward scene. I encouraged the representative. Still stunned at what just happened, she thanked me.

I sat back down, put the headphones back in my ears, and looked around with a smirk I remember seeing on my daughter when she was three or four. There was no way I was going to just let him get away with treating someone else the way he did. I honestly feel sorry for him and hope he has found a healthy way to deal with his stress and anger issues.

That intervention was something just about anyone could have done. I wasn't uniquely gifted for the moment. I saw someone who needed help, and I chose not to ignore the situation but acted in the other person's best interest. Could I have ignored the situation? Yes. Could I have turned the volume up to drown out the conspicuous conversation? Absolutely! I chose to do something significant when I could have done a number of other things.

Every single person sitting there made a decision in that moment to ignore the opportunity to intervene. The same is true in life. There are people hurting all around us. Sometimes it's because of hunger, poverty, fear, or depression. There is someone not too far from where you are right now who needs your help.

What will your decision be? You're never too important to reach out and help someone else. Most of the time it doesn't cost you anything but a few words, a kind look, and a genuine smile. The irony is that for such a little sacrifice you might literally save a life.

> We only have one life to live, to give, and to offer as a blessing to others.

The Gospel According to Wayne

If there is one thing I want people to realize is that they have the ability to make a difference in the life of another person. It might be doing something you consider insignificant that helps someone else significantly overcome a moment of adversity and decide to fight another day.

When we find ourselves consumed with our desires, plans, and what benefits us, we miss the fact that there are hurting people all around us. They don't have to be poor and living on the streets . . .

Hurting people wear suits.
Hurting people drive nice cars.
Hurting people live in nice homes.
Hurting people work in a cubicle 9 to 5.
Hurting people can appear to have it all together.

Some have suggested to me that what I've done with Soles4Souls is more than they could ever dream of doing. The implication is that if you can't "go big," then stay home. Nothing could be farther from the truth. The better way to approach life is by recognizing the size of the difference has little to do with the size of the impact.

The size of the difference is not for us to judge. If someone is about to commit suicide because he or she believes no one in the world cares for him or her, then a small gesture of kindness may alter their plans. If someone is without shoes in a place where it is dangerously unhealthy not to have shoes, then a pair of shoes may save their life.

The size of the difference doesn't matter. The willingness to recognize the need in others to be loved, cared for, and made to feel valuable does. We have one chance to make a difference in the life of someone else. Will you embrace the opportunity now or reschedule it for another day?

Ten Minutes Early

I have a personal rule. I like to arrive at a place ten minutes early, especially if it is for a business meeting. I have learned that there is greater power in the expectation someone has walking toward you than in waiting for you to show up late.

I don't really have time to think too intently about pseudo power plays, but this one is always a fun experiment. Those who are prepared are glad to see me. Those who were hoping for a minute or two of preparation before I arrived wish they had stayed in their car just a few minutes longer.

A business associate and I were scheduled to meet with a third party. My associate knew my habit of arriving ten minutes in advance. He became worried as the meeting time arrived but I wasn't present. He politely excused himself to make a phone call. Just as he stood up, he noticed me coming toward the table and was relieved to know I had arrived. He later told me that I am so consistent that he worried something had happened. I guess you could say this habit of showing up ten minutes early has become part of my personal brand.

Each of us has a brand. We reinforce this brand by the decisions we make and the actions we take. When I decided to gather the courage I needed to respond to those helpless following the Asian tsunami, I didn't know where it would lead. I couldn't have anticipated the Katrina disaster soon to follow, and I would never have predicted that I would leave the comforts of my executive lifestyle to start a nonprofit that would exist to provide shoes to the shoeless.

Every time someone tells me how inspired they are by Soles4Souls, I remind them that they have the potential to achieve similar results. It starts with the decision to get off the couch, help others, and do something that matters. There is often a hint of disbelief in their eyes. For a few, it fuels their desire to build their wealth in hearts and lives of people. When you make a human connection with someone who needs what you have, sitting on the couch isn't good enough. When we know we have the potential to make a lasting difference with whatever we have, wherever we are, and in whatever ways we can, almost isn't good enough.

SEVEN

Look for Solutions Bigger than the Problem

"Most people spend more time and energy in going
around problems than in trying to solve them."
—Henry Ford

One of my executive staff members earned the position he
has today because he impressed me. It wasn't in an interview
or on the platform. It was a quick decision he made, which
helped Soles4Souls avoid a crisis I didn't even anticipate.

We were hosting a reception at a shoe industry event.
The reception was very well attended. We spent a great deal
of money on food, drinks, and creating the right atmosphere
because we needed this to be a memorable event. People
remember little when an event is positive, but they recall
every detail when the experience is anything less than what
they expected. We wanted to avoid the latter at all cost.

David had been in the hospitality and food service business for most of his career. He has worked in some of the most complex, demanding environments in the country. He quickly noticed that there were a growing number of half-empty trays sitting around the room. I had even thought to myself that we might have underestimated how much food we had purchased.

In a matter of moments, the half empty trays were gone. As I looked around the room, the trays had been carefully combined to give the appearance that we had actually brought out more food. As new attendees arrived, it appeared as if we had more than enough food for the event instead of running the risk of not having enough.

David gained my full respect that day. It never occurred to me to think about combining the trays. He never came and asked me what I wanted to do. He didn't leave the trays as they were. David knew that first impressions were everything, and he went the extra mile to ensure it was an unforgettable experience.

It was decisions like that one which earned him the position he has today as my executive vice president. He is the very kind of person that embodies what I hope to see in my entire team. The most important part of success is not knowledge but action.

problems come with solutions

One thing that irritates me more than anything else is when people come to me with problems without having thought through possible solutions. I would much rather someone come to me having thought through and even tested solutions when they reveal to me the challenges they are experiencing. So many organizations waste time talking about the problem when the focus should be on discovering the next steps.

I can't tell you the number of nonprofit leaders I meet who lament to me privately how many months it takes to get everyone on board before they can move forward. I've never understood why it should take so much energy to get a team looking and moving in the same direction. If that is a persistent issue, then it goes back to hiring the right people and empowering people to make decisions that move the ball down the field.

I do not have enough margin in my schedule to validate the problems people are having in their particular area of responsibility. What I do

> If I can't find you on Google, then you don't exist. Period.

have time for is helping them move the mountains they are already giving their blood, sweat, and tears to address. I will do everything in my power to remove the roadblocks that are preventing us from moving forward, but I will not sit around and wait as we define the problem at hand.

There is no problem without a solution. The solution may be completely crazy, and it may fail miserably. I'm not as interested in avoiding failure as I am in building a culture of work that values action more than perfection. The focus should not be on how to avoid problems as much as it should be on solving them.

Problems will come; that's guaranteed. The best we can do when those situations present themselves is look for the opportunity in the midst of the tension. Defining the problem is not the end goal, it's the starting point.

The HVAC Contractor

We recently moved into our new world headquarters just outside the city limits of Nashville, Tennessee. As with any construction project, there are always a lot of little things that need to be taken care of immediately following move-in day.

One unexpected surprise was that the building was not cooling as it should. We needed some additional insulation and HVAC equipment, so I asked my executive assistant to make sure the contractor was aware of our needs and to ask him to take care of it ASAP. I wasn't asking for anything free. I knew this was going to cost us a little extra, but it was an issue we simply couldn't afford to compromise on. Uncomfortable temperatures are the perfect storm of work distractions.

As usual, my schedule was packed with back-to-back meetings. I noticed a guy midmorning who was waiting patiently just down the hall from my office door. Each time I invited my next appointment into my office and then walked them out, he was still standing in relatively the same place.

I finally asked him how I could help. He started with a long explanation of what he had found, why the building wasn't cooling, and what we might have done differently. I stopped him a few paragraphs into the conversation and asked him how to fix it. He started rattling off several options of rearranging what was already existing. I asked him if that would fix it, and he said it would help.

It was at that moment I asked my next appointment to wait for just a second. I walked up to the guy and said, "Whatever you have to do to fix it, just fix it. If it costs me more, let me know how much. Most likely, I'll say yes." After a few seconds of silence, he started in again on possible fixes that might work. I told him that I was late for my appointment. I appreciated him being there, and I wanted him to fix it and get it right, but I didn't have time for trying things out. I told him again to just let me know what has to be done, how much it will cost, and I'll say yes.

He wasn't sure how to respond. I'm not sure what he thought about me, but I'm pretty sure I surprised him. As he walked away, I expressed my interest in having this work completed that day. He shook his head and smiled, knowing that there was no more conversation to be had. Instead, there was work to do. I think we both left the building that day much later in the evening than initially expected.

An advocate for the shoeless, a partner with the Donor

One way to constantly keep focused on solutions that are bigger than your problems is to make sure you remain an advocate for the people you can help by partnering with your donors. Without donors, your organization or cause is paralyzed at the point in time you max out your internal mission capacity.

There are three hundred million children in the world without shoes. The better we are at partnering with our donors, the more people we can help. I spend very little time thinking about what similar nonprofits are doing. My competition is not other nonprofits but the race against the clock to give away as many shoes as possible for as long as I can.

Partnering with donors focuses your efforts to create solutions that make it easy for the donor to interact with Soles4Souls using their preferred means of communication, not mine. I need to spend more time learning about my donors than worrying about what my donors think of me.

What are the preferences of my donors?
How do they want to interact with us?
What's most important to them?

One way we've recently adjusted to popular demand is by creating a mobile version of our Web site. (You should check it out: just punch "giveshoes.org" in your phone's mobile browser.) Did you know that more than 270 million Americans use cell phones, 42 percent being smartphones? That's just a few more donors than we have today.

The decision to go mobile was an easy one. It just made sense. We spent a few months making sure we put it together so in the end we'd have something our donors could actually use. While some nonprofits are still meeting about the last meeting to discuss the motion that will be voted on in an upcoming meeting, we spent our energy putting technology together to do something. The end result is a fully functional mobile site.

I wonder how many great ideas are surfacing in the midst of struggling and successful nonprofits that never see the light of day simply because they become buried in conversation and process. If you're the leader of a nonprofit and you sense this is going on, then you have to ask yourself what's more important: process and procedure, or impact and problem solving?

The quick answer is impact and problem solving. No one wants to admit that it is process and procedure. If our work as leaders is to lead and solve problems, then we must not spend our energy making decisions but putting them into action.

I wonder what has been tabled for discussion that needs to be acted upon so you can spend your energy and efforts on expanding the level of donor engagement and finally solving the problems your organization or cause exists to ultimately eliminate.

Five Problems with Your Nonprofit

I get frustrated with nonprofit leaders maybe more than I should. The reason is they should know better. I have little patience with some of them who seem so consumed with the wrong things. It's no wonder donors have a bad taste in their mouth when anyone claiming to be from a nonprofit shows up on the screen of their TV, computer, or smartphone.

There are three parts to every task: problem, solution, and urgency. Most nonprofits are great at outlining the problem. Many are good at creating a sense of urgency. Few have a plan to eliminate the source of the problem. This is why so many nonprofits fade into the background of good intentions instead of standing out by declaring that almost isn't good enough.

If we aren't presenting solutions, then nonprofit leaders are simply performers who know how to create a particular emotion within their audience, which leads people to give or support the organization or cause through manipulation. I'm certainly not suggesting that emotion should not be present, but what I don't understand is why our emotion doesn't lead to action.

Here are five problems (i.e., things you may hear donors saying) that nonprofit leaders should solve to increase their footprint and success rate:

1. *"I can't find you online."*

It still amazes me how many nonprofits still aren't making investments in their digital presence. If you haven't modified your Web site in the last thirty days (no, ten days), then you are out of date. If you haven't allocated money to contract with (or hire) someone who knows digital Web design, then you are missing out on the chance to engage with people in a credible way. If I can't find you on Google, then you don't exist. Period.

2. *"I don't understand what you do."*

A good rule of thumb is if you can't recite the mission of your organization, then you have no hope of spreading the message and funding your work. What problem are you solving? How are you solving it? How can I help? The answer to those three questions are the basis of any great organization. Remember the key elements of every task: problem, solution, and urgency.

3. *"It's difficult to get more information."*

Please don't make me give you my address in order to send me information in the mail. I'm not patient enough for that. Once I realize that you want to mail me something, I'm moving on to another nonprofit Web site. This isn't a matter of minutes but seconds. I don't mind giving you my address when I'm ready, but I should be able to learn everything I need to know and feel as though I can trust you without giving you personal information.

4. *"It's impossible for me to get involved beyond giving money."*

Every organization is looking for money. I don't care if you are a for-profit or a nonprofit. Just asking me to donate doesn't differentiate you from anyone else. Why not ask me to join you in your work, then I'll decide if you are worthy of my donations? Every leader should be asking, How can we get more people involved so they can see the pain in the lives of those we are trying to help? When I do that, I move from being an interested party to a raving evangelist.

5. *"I never hear from you except when you want me to give."*

If our relationship is based on you asking and me giving with little to no additional interaction, then we don't have much of a relationship. Leaders must choose to drive their organizations to be organization-centric or donor-centric. If you are organization-centric, then your greatest concern is asking me for more dollars. If you are donor-centric, then your relationship strategy will center on helping me fulfill my dreams and passion of making a difference in the world through your organization.

Irrelevance isn't a plague or plight thrust upon you. I've grown weary of hearing nonprofit leaders citing the reason for their lack of volunteers, progress, impact, and funding on everything except their unwillingness to push through their excuses instead of using them like a crutch.

Relevance is the result of the type of organization you've created, the investments you make with what you've been given, and a stubborn commitment to the donor.

The speed of solutions

When the Haiti earthquake hit, we were absolutely over-whelmed with the response of our donor base, which was interested in working through Soles4Souls to provide some relief and aid to those hurting in that very poor country. We operate with a lean staff, so we didn't have a huge call center to manage all the inquiries. Every single one of us in the office began taking calls in addition to the workload we currently had. I quickly realized the demand was not dimin-ishing, so we needed to find a way to channel those calls in a way that helped us connect with the person on the phone and allowed my staff to focus on our response grounded in their specific area of expertise.

After making a few phone calls, we found a call center that was open to my management training them to make sure the callers' experience was similar to what they would experience were they to call our office directly. This was an expensive decision but absolutely necessary. The only way we were going to put together a plan that would work was to ensure my team was free to gather the details and form a plan of action.

Before Haiti, we were running at fifty-five miles per hour and comfortable with our pace. In just one week, it felt as if we were moving at two hundred miles per hour. At that speed, an inability to make decisions and focus on solutions leads to a frightful end where everything comes apart. Instead, our bent toward problem solving and action became a centrifuge that created a wave of momentum that has propelled us forward in ways no one could have anticipated, expected, or predicted.

Giving away shoes to people who don't have them is really a matter of life and death. I was fully aware that every day Haitians would contract fatal diseases and needlessly expose themselves to infection and a host of other medical challenges if they had no way to protect their feet from the ground. There was no time for meetings to define the problem. We already knew why we existed. We needed every available ounce of energy directed at creating a solution that was bigger than the problem.

stay in the game

Our goal is not to give a hand out but a hand up. A transaction in a retail store makes a sustainable difference in the lives of others. The associate keeps his or her job, the manager continues to grow the business, the corporate structure is able to invest in new products and promotions, and the consumer has access to the product or service they had been looking to purchase.

Transactions create revenue. Revenue creates margin. Margin supports the organization's ability to stay in the game long enough to make a sustainable difference. When the solution is bigger than the problem, the organization or cause gets to come back the next day and do it all over again. It's not about a great first effort but being vibrant and healthy enough to put into action the second, third, and fourth effort.

There is no such thing as a perfect solution. If there was, there is no way we could know it going forward. While there is a great deal of clarity as we reflect back over situations, moving forward at a rapid pace means accepting failure and still moving forward. What happens as we look for solutions larger than the problem is that we find a way to stay in the game until we get it right.

The secret to all of this can be summed up in one sentence: Go through life with your hands open. Remember that whatever cause or organization you subscribe to or lead is not yours to possess. The present is a moment in time when you are afforded the opportunity to make a difference. The only chance we have at achieving a measurable impact is to do something.

In the midst of our doing, we will stumble into unexpected pitfalls, experience unanticipated obstacles, and grow frustrated at our inability to do more. Yet it is also in the doing that we have the chance to give away enough of ourselves to be reminded that the most important treasure in life is buried within the human connection.

This is why we must avoid the temptation to become stagnant as we spend too much time defining the problem. Instead, we must accept the challenge of responding to the urgent, demanding, endless cry from those we are able to help.

Progress Only comes Through Action

"In a moment of decision, the best thing you can do is
the right thing to do. The worst thing you can do is nothing."
—Theodore Roosevelt

Our international headquarters is in Nashville, Tennessee.
That is also where I live. It is a great "little-big" city that has
grown on me over the years. I was driving around town one
day when I noticed for the first time people selling newspapers on street corners. This was not an uncommon site when
I was growing up in Virginia, but we live in a time when
traditional media, especially newspapers, are suffering. How
could they possibly afford to pay people to stand on street
corners and sell copies of the newspaper?

Being the curious person that I am, I rolled down the
window and asked one individual about the newspaper he

had for sale. The kind man, who clearly hadn't showered in a day or two, told me that this paper was written, produced, and sold by homeless people to provide for their needs. He told me if he sold a certain number every day then he would no longer have to be homeless. I could tell from his eyes that he believed it could happen—and probably knew at least one or two people who had risen above homelessness by selling, of all things, newspapers. I gladly paid him the one dollar.

I took the time to read his newspaper and was blown away by how something so simple could have such a profound impact on someone's life. Further, it underlined for me that people would much rather be given a hand up than a hand out. This guy was proud to be selling these newspapers. I imagine he woke up early, knew the best spots and the peak times to distribute enough newspapers to earn his way out of homelessness, and worked until he sold all that he needed to for the day.

If this could work for people in the United States, why couldn't it work around the world?

A Different kind of shoe Retailer

One morning it occurred to me that we could do something similar to the selling of newspapers but related to the distribution and sale of shoes. Here is how it works: we provide shoes to local people in need of work who essentially function as retailers. They sell these shoes in their community and are able to keep what they earn. These individuals, for the first time, are able to earn enough to buy food for their families, send their children to school, and provide for their well-being. It's called a microbusiness model, and it's working.

Before we launched into it, there were countless people who told me why it wouldn't work. Some had lots of letters behind their names and had done a lot of important things in life. Some had positions of authority and led well-known organizations. Nonetheless, many people told me I was absolutely crazy and were certain it would never work. (If you haven't figured it out by now, when someone tells me no I use it as an incentive to make it work.)

I knew we already had the capacity to collect and distribute shoes. That was our core business. The only additional element was finding the interested individuals and building a vendor relationship with them. It wasn't rocket science. I knew that the same passion that inspired the homeless man to sell newspapers to escape his present condition was part of the human spirit and not just a local phenomenon.

A New Kind of Nonprofit

What surprises me the most is that a microbusiness doesn't depend upon the free will giving of others. It doesn't create and perpetuate a group of people dependent upon a wealthier demographic to survive. It empowers individuals to discover their potential to do more than they first thought possible through their own efforts. There is no amount of charity that can offer the kind of dignity and self-respect that comes from earning your own way.

One of the most frustrating things about the nonprofit world is that many in this arena aren't looking for solutions. Therefore, too many nonprofits stall out in the decision-making process instead of pushing through the unknowns to define and implement a plan of action. It is better to fail miserably than to work hard at preventing failure but never act on anything.

We live in a new time with a new kind of donor, one that demands greater amounts of information and to see measurable impact being made. The new donor is not dependent upon the organization to tell them about the organization but comes with well-researched questions and expectations that the organization must be prepared to address directly and honestly.

The new kind of nonprofit will be driven by action. The annual rubber chicken dinner and fall gala just won't cut it anymore (more on that in a moment). Sustainability is at the forefront of everybody's mind. What we are doing today is just as important as what we will be doing five years from now. If almost isn't good enough in the light of the problems we champion and people we serve, then the actions we take must move us closer to solving problems and making a difference.

Too Much Work

Not everyone handles the type of responsibility handed to each of the team members at Soles4Souls. It is literally overwhelming for some who are not ready to create their own paths and would, instead, prefer to have someone tell them what to do and when. We don't have time for that. As you have probably caught on by now, I'd much rather someone try and fail than to not have tried at all.

That means we stay until the work is done, not when the work day ends. That means we wake up early or work weekends if necessary. It's not about fulfilling a job description. More importantly, it's about being part of the solution. The only way to submerge yourself into the solution is to become a part of the action.

The days of Dad coming home early and Mom having dinner ready on the table are quickly fading if not completely over. One parent is coming home late after an impromptu meeting with executive management while the other parent is busy balancing the crammed extracurricular schedules of two children and completing a big client project themselves.

The problem is that some nonprofits aren't living in the real world. They aren't in touch with the everyday demands of real life enough to appeal with any sense of authenticity to the average donor. Leaders want to continue doing the same old, tired things and hope for better results year after year.

I am asked frequently about how we structure our annual fundraising dinner. I tell them we don't have a dinner. When they ask why, I tell them it's because I don't like rubber chickens. They walk away offended when that wasn't my intention. I don't like rubber chickens any more than my donors do, so why would I ever consider that as a viable strategy to raise funds and make a difference.

In the new world of organizational funding and building mission capacity, action requires that we break the traditional boundaries when necessary to accomplish the stated goal. The nonprofit world should exist to solve problems and create solutions, not perpetuate the existence of the organization so we can continue to exist in our comfortable little corners of the world at the expense of those we exist to help.

Action Begins with Listening

Our current Web presence is miles from where we started in the digital space. We were so excited about what we were doing and so eager to prove that we were worthy of donations that we dumped just about every piece of information we had onto our Web site. The result was excessive clutter that was unappealing to the eye and ineffective at getting us the traction we needed.

I reached out to a friend who I knew excelled in helping his clients navigate the digital space and had success helping organizations like ours reinvent their digital presence. He had some difficult words for me to hear. We were going to have to make some significant changes and a complete overhaul of the entire site was not out of the question.

We had spent a lot of time getting our Web presence up and running. In my opinion, it wasn't a bad site. But I recognized that what my friend was telling me would lead to a level of digital engagement that I hadn't even considered. I made a quick decision to adopt the strategy he was suggesting. I didn't wait to meet with my board of directors. I didn't gather the team together and ask everyone to weigh in on the decision. We didn't need more conversation—we needed to take action and make this happen. I knew

> Failure is not a bad thing. It is an opportunity to learn something.

that our digital presence would be key to our future success and would soon become the preferred way for the new donor to interact and engage with Soles4Souls.

Focus on Business Development

I'm convinced that not enough nonprofits live in the tension between their present capacity and the sense of urgency to provide relief for those they exist to serve. The job of an executive director is not to perpetuate programs but to provide solutions and lead their organizations to take action.

An organization that is focused on business development is never satisfied with the status quo. They are always striving for something greater, the next big win that will move the ball down the field and a little closer to making a significant difference.

When leaders look for new places to invest the assets given by donors, the first step should be developing a business plan. In the culture of Soles4Souls, we call those one-sheeters. Every new idea has to have a one-sheet overview before it can be considered.

In case you're wondering, there is significance to having one-sheeters. We don't do anything without purpose. It's easy to bury important details when you are putting large amounts of data together. I'm not interested in being impressed by a team member's ability to think, reason, and create. I wouldn't have hired them if I didn't believe they embodied those characteristics. In the same way that it's easy to compile large amounts of data together, it is an even more complicated discipline to reduce an entire business concept to one page.

I'm not a fan of meetings, and I travel too much to spend the precious hours I am in the office listening to everyone pontificate about ideas specifically related to their side of the business. If progress and action are my litmus test of credibility, then I only want to interact with those team members who believe enough in their idea to do a mountain of research and condense that into a business plan that can be found on one sheet of paper.

If we don't push ourselves to constantly look for ways to expand our capacity, then we risk becoming the type of nonprofit organization we never wanted to be. The same can be said about our individual lives. When we stop learning, growing, and exploring, there is a part of our being that dies. We settle into the mundane and accept that this is all there is to life. It's time to wake up and move in a direction that will reignite the passion to do something significant and build a legacy to be remembered in the hearts and minds of those we have the ability to help.

Action Often Leads to Failure

I can't for the life of me understand why failure is feared so greatly by nonprofit leaders. When you take risks, you have to accept failure. Not every idea at Soles4Souls works, even if it makes it to a one-sheeter. No one expects it to. What's important is that if you fail because you took action, then you are at least one step further in your journey to making a lasting impact than you were before.

We have a few members on the team who are into running as an exercise and hobby. Road races have become very popular over the last thirty years. Running has also become a popular way nonprofits have found to raise funds. We decided to try our hand at this growing option.

We knew we didn't want to get into race management, so we decided to model another nonprofit's very successful approach to engaging people to train together in groups and race together for a common cause. We were confident we could engage others already participating in this sport. We did everything we knew to do, and it failed miserably. We eventually had to pull back and cancel the effort completely.

But that's not where the story ends. It was now our job to figure out what went wrong and what we could learn from it. Two important things surfaced in the midst of our evaluation. One, this was outside our core competency. It is important to make sure we keep the main thing the main thing. We must be strong in the ways where we know we have strength. Two, Soles4Souls was not as well-known when we launched this concept as we thought. That was brutal to admit, but it revealed an opportunity for us to re-examine our communication strategy.

We would never have discovered those two things had we not taken the risk in the first place and then taken the time to understand what went wrong and what went right. Failure is not a bad thing. It is an opportunity to learn something.

Action sometimes Leads to a surprising Discovery

Another idea that made its way to a one-sheeter became a huge, unexpected success. It would later be name Barefoot Sunday. We were looking for a way to engage churches in shoe collections, beyond what we were already doing by providing donation boxes they could put in their foyers. We helped them by providing materials to distribute and planning a special emphasis upon request. We'd had moderate success but knew there was more potential than what we were currently accessing.

The idea was to help churches make an event out of a simple shoe collection. What if we encouraged church leaders to challenge their members to bring shoes and leave them at the altar? We knew a few churches would pick up on the idea quickly. What we didn't anticipate was the number of churches that took this opportunity very seriously. It wasn't long after we launched this initiative that we began to see videos post online, letters from people moved by the experience, and church leaders more interested than ever in ways they could partner with Soles4Souls.

It was definitely a success. Who would have thought that such a simple idea as bringing shoes and leaving them at the altar would have such a profound effect on members? When I've had the chance to see this first hand, it occurred to me that the greatest testimony was not only in the hundreds of shoes left at the foot of the platform but the hundreds of people leaving church that Sunday morning with no shoes on. This simple act of solidarity and generosity is absolutely overwhelming.

Take the challenge

I meet a lot of people who confess that they want to make a difference but don't know where to begin. They find excuses in their age, education, gender, life circumstance, and any number of things. I also meet a lot of nonprofit leaders who live with the frustration of having a passion to lead their organizations in new ways but feeling captive to a culture that doesn't tolerate failure or make room for risk.

As much as I want to sympathize with both groups, I keep coming back to the personal decision we all must make to live the life we have been given. Don't blame anyone or anything but yourself if you choose not to make a difference. Every day I get up with the image of those around the world I've met who are dying because of diseases they contracted, which might have been completely avoided by having shoes on their feet. When I think about those people, I lose patience with any reason anyone might give to justify their decision to pass on opportunities because the cost was too great.

Action is scary. It is not for the weary or the faint of heart. It requires discipline, forethought, initiative, and the acceptance that failure may be the end result. The older I get the more convinced I am that some people can handle this pressure and some people can't. What I refuse to tolerate are people who try to pretend they want to help when all they really want is to feel better about themselves. While a portion of the world dies, we fight over how we are going to split the donor dollars we have received. In doing so, we don't solve any problems and ignore the very reason for our existence.

Stop making excuses and start making it happen. Choose today to be the first day with your fresh agenda and a renewed passion for impact and results. Try something. Fail. Learn. And do it all over again. If those of us who have the capacity and margin to become advocates for others in need do not create progress through action, then we have sealed the fate of the helpless and abdicated our responsibility to do something meaningful.

Just like the homeless man selling newspapers as his way to earn a ticket to a more stable existence, we also have the chance to extend the same opportunity to others around the world who weren't fortunate enough to be born into our families, receive our education, and have access to the most basic human needs. Soles4Souls does this by providing shoes to the shoeless. I wonder what can be found in the margin of your life that could change the course of another almost instantly.

Almost is never good enough.

obsess over the numbers

"High achievement always takes place in the
framework of high expectation."
—Charles Kettering

I learned early in my career that in numbers people can discover . . . and in numbers is the substance by which leaders
can validate key decisions and justify sizable organizational
investments of time, energy, and people.

As I mentioned in an earlier chapter, at one point in my
career I was responsible for repairing ailing retail locations. My
job would be to assume the role of store manager at a particular site and attempt to uncover why it was not performing at
or above projected levels. In most cases, corporate was trying
to determine whether to shut down or repurpose these stores.

I remember one store at which the constant complaint registered with corporate's quality department was that people were waiting too long to be fitted and purchase shoes. I couldn't understand why that was the case. It was rare that stores were not staffed at a level that could easily handle regular traffic.

After investigating the work schedules alongside the times and dates linked to the complaints, it became apparent that the answer was not to hire more employees but to do a better job scheduling their hours. After a few weeks of observing the traffic flow, I was finally able to get a handle on the shopping habits of our customers. Then I mapped our work schedules around peak customer traffic times. The result was an almost immediate elimination of registered complaints with corporate. My job was complete.

Had I not investigated the data available to me, I might have been inclined to react as most managers would and hire more people. That decision would have been the most expensive solution to fix the problem, which would have accelerated the financial decline of the location. Instead, we avoided needless hiring and improved the fiscal stability of the location.

It was during such experiences that I learned to rely less on my intuition and more on the data to point out the source of a problem and to let me know whether we were healthy or simply postponing a disaster.

Intuition Is Not a Good Strategy

Each week I receive a one-page overview of a few key metrics that let me know how we are doing as an organization. This report has been instrumental in our ability to recalibrate as needs have shifted. I remember after one national tragedy, our phone began ringing off the hook. Every single one of us, including me, was answering calls from donors interested in learning how they could get involved and offer relief through Soles4Souls.

It was getting to the point where none of us could get any work done. When we looked at commitments we had made for the near future and the reality that there seemed to be no diminishing interest from our donors, we determined that we needed reinforcements so our team could focus on the necessary tasks to keep the organization moving forward.

During this time we also noticed more than one-fourth of our incoming phone calls were from people looking for the closest donation point. After speaking with my marketing director, we determined that we needed to highlight that section of our Web site. In less than twenty-four hours we had made the change and the calls associated with that request virtually disappeared. We would never have known to make these adjustments had we not been paying attention to the numbers.

My Obsession, Their Affirmation

In addition to the one-page overview with key metrics, I receive individual reports weekly from every area of Soles4Souls. I know what's going on, what's working, and what isn't. I'm thrilled to receive this because it gives me a reason to look for ways to affirm people's efforts. I know it sounds strange how numbers can actually be used to create and solidify an emotional connection, but it's true.

When my employees know that I pay attention to their work, notice their specific contribution, and then brag on them, it shows that I care. I'm traveling a lot these days. My days start before the sun goes up and ends well after the sun goes down. My time in the office is usually booked since I only have limited time available to meet with employees and other people and organizations. That means I must make an extra effort to ensure every one of my employees knows that I care about them and am proud of their work.

It's one thing to tell people that you like them. It's another thing to recognize someone for starting a new venture that has been immensely more successful than first anticipated or brag on a quiet personality in the accounting area who saved us thousands of dollars by discovering a few incorrect invoices from vendors.

When you hire the best, it's vitally important that they hear the leader affirm their work. It's tough to be the employee working hard and thinking no one even cares that you're working this hard. It's tough being the boss when you have so much on your plate and, even with the best of intentions, you never seem to have enough time to praise those who are going above and beyond to make things happen. Numbers provide the perfect flow of excuses to tell the people who work for you just how great they are. (Hint: It will pay huge dividends.)

Numbers Focus Our Efforts

Achieving anything measurable in life, business, or whatever means having an obsession with numbers or data, which offers objective feedback. Some people can handle it while others are paralyzed by it. Sometimes even highly qualified and well-suited people don't last long at Soles4Souls because they can't operate at a high speed and with the constant reminder that results matter.

When we rely only on ourselves as the primary source of wisdom and strength to achieve a larger-than-life goal, then we limit our potential to our context, experience, and ability. Instead, we must be willing to ask questions, learn from others, and seek out help when appropriate.

I remember when we moved one step closer to our overall goal of giving away a pair of shoes every second by moving from one pair given every nine seconds to one pair given every seven seconds. Such a measurable moment lets us know we are doing our best and directing our energy and resources to the best people and in the right areas. We would not have been able to achieve this step if we didn't measure our efforts and rely on each other to get there.

Budgeting: My Favorite Time of Year

It may sound absolutely crazy for me to say this, but one of my favorite times of the year is budget time. Given my past experience in some organizations, I understand that the word budget has a lot of excess baggage associated with it. As a salesperson, I fought against it. Once I became the chief executive, I saw it as a tool to direct our organization. The mistake many people make is thinking the organization was created for the budget when the budget was, in fact, created for the organization.

Our approach to budgeting is much different from most organizations. It begins with the senior leadership coming together and asking, Where are we today? and Where do we want to be in twelve months? I get to hear stories of impact as well as hear some of the most talented people passionately and thoughtfully share how they want to invest in certain areas.

We celebrate the progress we have made and define what will be our benchmark moving forward. The budget allows us to be the best we can be and offers a plan for us to take the next step as an organization that will ultimately increase our capacity to give away more shoes.

When you start with questions about what's next, you change the conversation and the atmosphere in the room. All of a sudden the discussion centers around what's possible instead of what's reasonable. Too many good ideas have been sacrificed for the sake of reason when they should have been released into the open spaces of possibility.

Numbers Speak Loudly

Around where I live, I am beginning to see signs from hospitals advertising the current waiting time in their emergency rooms. If I need medical attention outside my primary care physician's office, wouldn't I make my decision based on the shortest available wait time? Sure I would.

The same is true for organizations. Business is basically a series of cycles going up and down. You can't always assume that good things will continue to be good forever or that bad times will have no end. A good organizational leader accounts for both during any given period of time. If we pay attention to the cycles, we discover the data we need to make informed decisions moving forward.

For example, if we noticed that revenue over the past ninety days is less than what was projected, it's time to make adjustments over the coming ninety days until we have new information to suggest that we are back on track. The balance sheet becomes a business partner and trusted advisor whenever we need to make tough organizational decisions.

One of the consequences of a recession is that it reveals the true health of an organization. Too many nonprofits assumed that year-over-year growth would continue forever. They built their budgets around this trend and incurred expenses based on revenue streams that wouldn't last forever. When the money stopped flowing—or at least stopped flowing so freely—their poor financial health was revealed. If sustainability is the goal, then it becomes crucial to ensure that the organizations we lead are financially viable in both good and bad economic times.

> When you hire the best, it's vitally important that they hear the leader affirm their work.

confidence in consistency

One reality of leadership that most people never see, experience, or understand is how a leader always carries his or her organization. It becomes your new shadow. You realize that people are depending on you for paychecks and decisions internally, your donors are trusting you to make good on your promises to them that earned their donation, and, perhaps most important, the people who will benefit from your organization or cause are relying on your help to survive. That's a lot of pressure.

Being out of the office is tough for someone like me who enjoys rolling my sleeves up and getting in the details. I've had to learn over the years that I must let go and empower the people who work for me. When I receive my weekly one-pagers and see that all signs are good, it gives me confidence in my team's ability to perform consistently and manage well. This frees me to invest in areas such as business development, strategic partnerships, and forging new ground and initiatives that will carry the work forward toward an even greater impact.

There is no greater tool for a leader than the analytical data that validates good decision making and consistent performance. Still, I'm surprised by how many nonprofit leaders know very little about how to use numbers to their advantage. It's as if they apply their own personal money management habits to organizational theory and expect it to work in the same way. I speak with many nonprofit leaders who believe that if revenue is coming in at a certain level then the organization is healthy. There is never an acknowledgment that they understand how it has happened or whether this is a trend they see continuing through the coming quarter, six months, or year.

Obsessing over the numbers is the primary management tool necessary to keep an organization or cause in the game long enough to definitively substantiate the difference they are making in the world. It's not sexy, but it is the eyes and ears a leader needs to create a level of consistency that resonates with current donors and invites others to invest in you.

Financials Aren't the Only Numbers That Matter

We've talked a lot about financials. These are absolutely important metrics to measure and to justify making adjustments to core strategies. But financials aren't the only numbers that matter. At Soles4Souls, here are some numbers that matter to us:

- *1 Billion—Estimated number of people who do not own a pair of shoes.*
- *994—Number of nonprofit and government agencies in the U.S. and around the world that partner with Soles4Souls to distribute shoes.*
- *125—Number of countries where the charity has delivered shoes.*
- *250,000—Amount of shoes collected for victims of the Asian tsunami of 2004.*
- *1 Million—Amount of shoes distributed to survivors of Hurricane Katrina.*
- *300 Million—Estimated number of children around the world who do not own a single pair of shoes.*
- *2,133—Number of churches, synagogues, and mosques that have participated in shoe drive events.*
- *12 Million—The number of shoes distributed by Soles4Souls.*
- *1—The number of people it takes to give, distribute, or receive shoes.*

These numbers describe the great need that offers us the motivation to keep pressing forward. These numbers provide the evidence that our investments are paying out measurable dividends and making a difference. The most powerful number listed above, in my opinion, is the last number listed—1. We must never underestimate the power of one person to change the life of another through the simple act of giving, distributing, and receiving shoes.

To the critics

I am fully aware of a small yet irritating group of nonprofit leaders that oppose any effort to operate a nonprofit like a for-profit entity. They oppose any idea of establishing metrics with the argument that it taints the purity of the effort. Another small group of critics justify not paying attention to the numbers, citing that it is not part of their skill set. They leave that for the accountants and board to wrestle with. Both groups are wrong.

Leaders like me operate with the belief that by obsessing over the numbers, we can ensure that we are making a greater, longer-lasting impact, which will ultimately lead to transformational change. To any would-be critics, I want to offer you some things to think about:

Don't write a check you can't cash. It only harms the nonprofit world and contributes to the jaded donor when organizations and causes can't deliver on their promises. Reputation is key. Even the best of intentions can be crushed if you have to go back on your promises. There are countless examples in our culture. I want to be clear that there is a difference between trying something and failing and committing to something that was never going to happen.

That is why it is vital that no commitments come out of your mouth without testing it internally. Work your idea out on paper. Show it to a few trusted advisors. Meet with key donors, but don't try to be a hero. While there may be some instances where the impossible happens, you can't build a sustainable effort on miracles.

Never overcommit to anything. This would include time, money, or emotions. You'll end up overdrawn. Soles4Souls started as a simple response to one tragic event. I didn't try to function like the international relief organization we are today when the Asian tsunami hit in 2004. Had I tried that approach, my idea would have failed miserably and Soles4Souls would likely never have taken shape.

Be realistic from the beginning. Whether it's one small act of kindness or a big, audacious goal, don't expect to change the world in one day. Do what you can where you are today. Whether you are an organization or an individual, adjust your expectations. It's easy to read a book like this or listen to an inspiring speaker and want to change the world in one night. If you attempt that, you'll end up burning out, and the world will never discover the goodness you have to offer.

Give yourself a break. Making a difference is serious work. While it may be grounded in passion and emotional experiences, often your work will be conducted when you feel as though your tank is half empty. It's OK to have days when you're ready to give up.

Let me tell you a secret: there are times when I think what we are doing has reached an end. When I feel like this, I will drive over to the parking lot of another organization and wonder what struggles they are going through, what pressures they are dealing with, and what questions they are striving to answer.

It's during those times that I'm reminded every organization has problems. It is not unique to Soles4Souls. Not that I find solace in the struggles of others, but I am reminded that every organization, every cause, every effort brings with it its own set of challenges that ask us to reach deep within to find the strength to continue. The good news is that when I fear the worst, I am often surprised with very good news. I'm continually amazed how our impact continues to increase and our capacity expands.

Numbers are not the enemy. They can become the strength and confidence we need to know that our personal investment is worthy of our time, talent, and treasure. They can also become the motivation we need to make one more phone call to one more donor to get the support we need to move forward with our next important initiative. Just because numbers are not native to your context, doesn't mean they don't matter.

Obsess over the numbers. This discipline will make you grow, challenge you, and provide the substance and evidence of what you know, deep within, to be true.

TEN

No More Excuses

"If you don't want to do something,
one excuse is as good as another."
—Yiddish Proverb

So I'm walking through the middle of Times Square in New York City when I see this guy holding a sign. This isn't my first trip to NYC. I know there are a few crazy people in just about every major city, especially this one. Nevertheless, I had to know what it said.

I was far enough away when I first noticed the sign that I couldn't decipher what it said, no matter how much I squinted or strained my eyes. As I got closer, I couldn't believe what I was reading. The sign said, "Free Hugs."

Brilliant! was the first word that came to mind.

I approached the young guy, asked him about the poster

and if he was really there to give people hugs. He responded with a resounding "Yes!"

Maybe this guy was just plain crazy. I had to find out why, so I asked him if there was a particular reason he was doing this. Had he lost a bet with his fraternity brothers? Was this one of those secret camera shows?

He didn't miss a beat as he explained that he comes to the city mainly on the weekends when he has free time and offers free hugs to people who want them.

I was, to say the least, impressed.

This experience reminded me it doesn't take a college degree, keys to the executive suite, or even money to make a difference in the life of someone else.

I wonder how many people will laugh, how many will feel important, and how many will resolve to pay it forward through another act of kindness because one guy, one stranger, took the time to give them a hug.

This guy is changing the world with a poster and the balance of some free time on the weekends. What's your excuse?

The Motivation of No

It sounds strange to say it, but I believe one of the reasons Soles4Souls has been so successful is because we've endured a world of no. From the very beginning, there were people who were absolutely convinced that we wouldn't amount to anything other than a flash in the pan.

Every time I run into those people, I am reminded of what Mrs. Busch told me so many years ago when she gave me permission to believe in myself and the impossible. That's what I have done.

My greatest disappointment is to hear leaders talk about the defeat they find in the word no. They are too quick to give up on their dreams. They are inspired, work toward creating a viable plan, and then completely abort the process at the first sign of distress.

In chapter 8, we talked about the one-sheeter that each team member prepares when he or she is ready to share a new plan of action or area in which to invest. The rest of the story is those one-sheeters don't stay clean, white sheets of paper. They are marked up, erased, rewritten, and reworked until a good, solid idea becomes a great idea that is ready to be tested.

I would challenge individuals and organizations to see the word no as an opportunity to break new ground and try something different. If no is the worst someone can tell you, the best that could happen is for you to find a way to prove them wrong.

Own Your Role

It's very easy for leaders to get into the habit of making decisions and setting priorities for others. This is especially true when you have a young workforce at the helm of your organization. Soles4Souls naturally attracts a lot of young talent. Young professionals want to be a part of what we are doing.

The easiest thing for me to do would be to tell them what to do. It would be simple to set our organization up so they would become mindless drones who only know how to articulate a question and execute my response. I choose to take an entirely different approach.

I want the people who work for me to set the agenda. This doesn't mean that the agenda they set is the final agenda. It means that I'm raising the level of expectation to include their ability to own their corner of the organization.

Those team members who accept this approach tend to set more aggressive timelines and goals than I would have set for them. What's even better is that they are much more likely to do what it takes to reach those goals if they own them.

If I were to set the agenda and timeline, it would stifle the conversation and disrupt the culture of Soles4Souls. I might even be viewed as a dictator instead of someone who is helping others reach beyond their current condition.

The Attitude of Others Can Become Yours

I enjoy being around people who are good at what they do. Even as the leader of Soles4Souls, I still voluntarily place myself in a position to learn from the experts. I want the rest of the organization to do the same.

It's important for me to build into the culture of Soles4Souls an atmosphere of how, not why. I learned long ago that the organization itself must exist beyond my personal capacity to direct its every move. I must rely on the strength of the team to carry the work forward. If I teach them to ask the right questions and help them to push through the objections, there is little tolerance for excuses and stagnate solutions.

It's true that you reflect the attitude of those who surround you. If the voices of your peers, boss, and clients are negative, then it will impact the way you view the world too. So often I find that team members who are quick to jump to excuses are the ones who are paying close attention to the naysayers in their world. They are also the ones that eventually find their way out of Soles4Souls, perhaps with a tinge of frustration.

Bill Gates was laughed at when he started talking about personal computers. Steve Jobs was criticized when Apple first introduced the iPod. And on more serious matters, many people have died for their ideas and their willingness to push beyond self-imposed limits for centuries. The best we can hope for is to look for people who will help us see beyond our excuses and support us along the way.

Your Message (and Messengers) Matter

Every member of my staff is a communicator. There are a few on my staff who are key communicators across a variety of platforms. When some organizations are eliminating professional communicator positions and cutting back on communication budgets, we are doing just the opposite. Why? Because content matters. Correction. Great content matters.

There is a great need for excellence in message creation and delivery. In fact, I would suggest that messaging is so important it ought to have a dollar value assigned to it. Our commitment to communicating the need and the opportunities for others to participate in the solution has made it easy for others to become aware of the problem, get involved, and expand our opportunity to change the lives of others around the world.

There are more than one million 501(c)(3) organizations in the United States alone. That's a lot of competing organizations broadcasting messages. Each one hopes to grab the share of mind and, ultimately, dollars needed for the organization to accomplish its stated goals or support its banner cause. So what happens when organizations don't communicate well? They get lost in the clutter and noise. Thus, we do and will continue to spend a sizable portion of our operating budget on powerful messaging.

Why should I spend time and money on messaging when I could direct it elsewhere? Here are a few ideas to consider:

Our donors want to hear from us. If our donors believe enough in what we are doing to send us money, organize a fund-raising event, or travel with us to distribute shoes, then they deserve to hear from us on a regular basis. It's not enough for them to hear from us when we want something from them. They are partners, not just providers, in the journey.

People need to be aware of the need. If we believe that what we are doing is worth investing our time, money, and careers, then it must be worth telling others so they can have the opportunity to join us in our efforts. The more people involved, the faster we reach our goal of distributing shoes to every person in need. We must work to ensure the need doesn't get lost in good intentions.

> **If *no* is the worst someone can tell you, the best that could happen is for you to find a way to prove them wrong.**

We are the voice of the shoeless. No one else is as close to the people in need of shoes as we are. I see the despair people have who need shoes but don't have access to them. I've watched people around the world stand in line for hours waiting for their first pair of shoes. It's our responsibility to be their voice. If we don't, who will?

I'm committed to investing in our message. It's worth at least one line item (maybe more) in our operating budget. Stop making excuses. Invest in your communication strategy, content, and technology. Is messaging something you fund adequately, or is it the first place you turn to make cuts?

The story you tell matters. If you want more people involved in the work, start telling better stories.

Ten Things I Want to Say to Every Nonprofit Leader

If I had the attention of every nonprofit leader, there are ten things I would say in hopes of moving beyond the endless flow of excuses and encourage them to begin thinking about ways to rethink what's not working and look for new, creative ways to produce results that make a measurable difference in the lives of others.

1. Be Absolutely Clear About Your Work

Think elevator pitch. You'll live and die by its brilliance or absence. Excuses keep you from doing the necessary work to discover what it is about what you do that makes you different, unique, and the best positioned to solve whatever social ill is at hand.

2. Surround Yourself with a Great Team

A leader, by definition, is someone who has followers. Don't fool yourself. You can't do it alone. You need others more than they need you. As you build this team, be sure to assemble it with people who share your same passion for the impossible.

Nonprofit work is about fighting against larger things than competition, bottom-line growth, and shareholder returns. It is an invitation to apply the same principles in a context that is far more emotionally taxing and intimate than any sales strategy might be in the for-profit world. The people you choose will either be consumed with excuses or use obstacles as launching pads to do something new and fresh.

3. Focus on Solving Problems

Nonprofit work is not about the pursuit of self-actualization. It is about the implementation of new ideas that result in a measurable difference. Excuses become an easy out when the entire conversation is about theory and philosophy. Putting the conversation in the midst of reality, implementation, and practical application asks you as the leader to craft a plan to create a better world rather than perpetuate a broken one.

4. Make a Decision

Be bold enough to make the call—and willing to accept the glory or suffer the consequences. If you're afraid to fail, then you already have. Too many people are counting on you to do something significant. Excuses will keep you from realizing just how much you can actually accomplish when you remove the barriers others impose upon you and your organization.

5. Believe Cash Is More than a Four-Letter Word

Don't be afraid of the subject of money. Ask for it with confidence. Cultivate it systematically. Money is the fuel you need to accelerate the implementation of your solution. Without money, you just have a good idea, and eventually the only thing you will produce is the rationalization that your cause or organization capitulated simply because the funding wasn't there. The reason you don't have the funding you need is because you are allowing your own excuses to hinder your fund-raising efforts.

6. Take Action
Being paralyzed by fear always leads to defeat. Taking risks sometimes will lead to your biggest successes. Know that each failure is one step closer to success. Screw up enough to get it right. Excuses inhibit action rather than encourage it.

7. Scale to the Size of the Need
Don't use a Band-Aid when you need stitches. Dream big. Then find a way to bring that dream into reality, even if it takes a lifetime. Nothing of great value is created in just one day. Don't operate within the framework that the only thing that exists is what you can see, taste, touch, and feel. Great things have been accomplished throughout history because leaders allowed themselves to see what was yet to be.

8. Check Your Numbers
Data doesn't lie. It's the best avenue available to a leader to objectively evaluate impact. Leaders are often emotionally involved, which may mean that you are blind to certain areas of your organization. Data doesn't lie. People do. Excuses soften the blow of the brutal facts and will also cause you to agree with your naysayers, who are convinced you can't overcome your obstacles. Don't let them win. Too much is at stake. Press on!

9. Adjust to Constant Chaos

The world is changing too fast to stay the same very long. If your strategy for success is building a system, setting it in motion, and then monitoring it on occasion to make sure all the parts are still moving, you've already failed. Chaos is the new normal. Instead of using disorder as an excuse not to do something, leverage the presence of chaos to be creative and discover new opportunities to accelerate the mission and impact of the cause or organization you lead.

10. Keep Your Eyes Looking Forward

Don't lament the past. Don't be consumed with the urgency of today. Keep your eyes looking ahead, anticipate what is next, and make appropriate adjustments along the way. Organizations and causes need leaders; museums need curators. There is a long tradition of people who have given up because they thought the task was too hard, the challenge too much, the risk too great. Choose to lead differently and watch a world of yes open to you.

Leave Excuses at the Feet of others

It's hard to be governed by excuses when we choose to live at the feet of others. I have very little patience with leaders who believe serving others is a job for someone else to do. They never miss a press conference, seminar gathering, or conference keynote. But when it comes to actually doing the work they are asking others to do, they are nowhere to be found.

I get a lot of criticism because Soles4Souls does things differently. We are as progressive as the rules will allow. Because we rock the boat, we sometimes become easy targets for those who don't want to see things in new ways.

There is one thing I'm committed to making sure no one can ever substantiate: that I am not part of the work we do. Every chance I get, I'm present at one of our shoe distribution events around the world. It's important to me for my team members to see me sweat alongside them as we put shoes on the feet of the shoeless. It is less an exercise in good management as it is a sign of solidarity and humility.

I've been sitting at the feet of others my entire career. It began the first time I knelt down to help a customer find the right-sized shoe. It continued as I rose through the corporate ranks. I was always intimately involved in the success and failure of whatever venture we were launching. I constantly looked for ways to help others be successful and achieve far more than they ever thought possible.

Today is no different. I am back at the feet of others as often as I have the chance, offering hope in the form of leather and laces. Those to whom we provide shoes are not the only ones who receive something during the transaction process. The unexpected reality is that when I put shoes on people's feet, I maintain a right-sized perspective about my life.

The most powerful position does not reside in the corner office suite. On the contrary, the most powerful position in life is found when we choose to serve others in need.

There is a strange thing that happens when we find ourselves serving others. We begin to look into the eyes of those who benefit from the work we do and realize that excuses are merely barriers to actually putting into action what we say is important. I have yet to meet a leader who is actively serving others and is paralyzed by excuses.

Quit worrying about the size of the impact. Whether it's a hug given freely to a stranger or holding the hand of someone as they take their last breath, there is no room for excuses in the midst of action. We are our own greatest critics. The greatest lie we can tell ourselves is that our excuses are anything more than manifestations of our own insecurities. The greatest opportunity we can afford ourselves is to ignore the critical voices around us and temper the voice within that is telling us no when life is handing us every reason to say yes.

ELEVEN

Get comfortable with chaos

"Chaos is a friend of mine."
—Bob Dylan

I touched on the topic of chaos in the previous chapter, but since it is so vital to the success of any organization, an entire chapter needs to be devoted to it. If you can embrace the chaos that surrounds and runs through your organization, you will be able to harness an energy that makes you stronger and takes you further than you ever imagined going.

One day we decided that we needed a way to connect more people to the shoe distribution process. Every team member who has actively given someone his or her first pair of shoes has been changed by that experience. We wondered if there might be people—whether or not they currently support us financially—who would be interested in seeing what Soles4Souls is all about.

This is not a new concept. In fact, major donors have been given these types of opportunities for years. Our idea was less a reward for a great amount that had been given as it was a new way to engage more people in our core work of giving away shoes. We believed people would even be willing to pay their own way. It wasn't going to "cost" the organization anything.

One of the realities of the new donor is that there is a growing interest to be on the front lines of the core work of an organization. Instead of that person already being part of the movement, some people are using this as a way to decide which organization to support. Others are looking for a new kind of vacation, if you will, one that allows them to get away and do some good. Either way, we knew that one day of onsite distributions would make a believer out of anyone willing to go with us.

We vetted the idea through our process described earlier in this book. It started as a one-sheeter, was marked up, and returned. It rose to the top again and was a strong enough idea that it survived all efforts to justify why we shouldn't do this.

The next step was to find a team member who would take responsibility for testing the effort. We weren't going to appoint a committee or add it to another person's plate. This wasn't an extra. Any idea worthy of investing in is worthy of appropriate staffing. We felt like one particular individual would help us get there. We found that one person, empowered her to execute with the resources needed for success, and told her to make it happen.

She did just that. She asked questions when she needed to. After each trip, she reasoned what went well and what could have been better. She made necessary adjustments. The net effect of her effort and our support is that each and every trip gets better and better.

All of this happened within a matter of a few months, not years, decades, or never.

one Definition of MBO

I never received formal business school training like some of the people who have that work for me. I do read a lot and am a constant learner. One term I picked up from Peter Drucker was MBO, or management by objectives.

The basic idea behind this now common business term is management defines its organization's core objectives to everyone so both management and non-management professionals understand what's important and what's not, what's valued and what's not, and what direction they are headed and which direction they are not. It's almost like a contract in that it sets expectations and provides boundaries within which the organization will operate.

Since my initial exposure to the concept, I thought it was an important one. I implemented it as a shoe executive, and it paid off in our ability to create an efficient, profitable business. When I started Soles4Souls, this was a for-profit business principle that I definitely wanted to translate into the language and practice of the nonprofit world.

I knew it would be a game-changing strategy. Each year we set what our goals and objectives will be. I would print them for you, but I won't for two reasons. One, you need to define what's important to you. Don't take your cue from me, look within. Two, there is nothing magical about our core objectives.

An Alternate Definition of MBO

I have come to use MBO in another way too. It describes the effect the core strategy of MBOs can have on an organization: to make better and outrageous. Each time we hit a goal, it's time to set another goal that is bigger, larger, and more daring than the first. Our ultimate goal is to put shoes on the feet of people who don't have them. But that isn't a goal you can wrap your arms around, so we look for small, more tangible goals to celebrate along the way.

I remember when we crossed the mark of giving away more than twelve million pairs of shoes. We had a live, real-time counter marking our progress on our Web site. Seeing that move toward twelve million created a level of excitement and energy that is hard to describe beyond a young child waiting for Santa to come on Christmas Eve.

As the numbers grew closer to the twelve million mark, we started preparing for it as if it were an event. I'm not referring to our corporate communications strategy or announcement schedule, I mean internally.

There was a growing sense that we were about to cross a mile marker that would be consistent with the core of who we were. When the announcement was finally made, everyone left their offices and celebrated in the halls. It was just one way we used our management by objectives strategy to make a better and outrageous organization that was getting traction and forging ahead.

The Implementation of MBO

We arrived at the five MBOs that we have in place (as of this writing) from a series of meetings among the executive management group. We didn't meet because it is our practice to do so, but because I wanted to be sure these were the right five that every area would take responsibility for and would, in fact, guide us to where we want to go.

Once we had agreed on the final five, each member of the executive team took a particular MBO and made it his own. This is how we organize in anticipation of the eventual chaos. Undirected energy is not healthy and doesn't create traction. We have a team of people passionate about what we do, highly skilled in their area of expertise, and who operate with a bias toward action. We knew that chaos already existed below the surface of these individuals; it's part of why we were drawn to them and them to us. Therefore, we decided to organize the chaos around the MBOs.

The great paradox is this: the best way to grow an organization or broaden an individual's impact is by gradually using the goals to provide direction without being tethered to structure, rules, and obligations. Different options are always available. There is more than one way to do just about anything. If the goal is defined, the process is negotiable. This will keep the high-achievement people who work for you interested and will ensure you are taking advantage of all the time and talent available to the organization.

> ❝ Changing the world means placing more emphasis on getting it done than on getting it right. ❞

An Open Door

My door is almost always open. I want people to know that I'm not simply issuing edicts from on high. I want them to see me forging new territory just as I'm asking them to do.

I've never understood why key organizational leaders lock themselves in executive suites and hide behind layers of management. I want to be with the people on the front lines because I want to be on the front lines. That is where the action takes place. It's not behind a desk or in meetings. It's when we break free of the office building crutch and remember that what makes us important is not the title on our business card but our willingness to do whatever it takes to help those we exist to serve.

I want people to see the level of intensity I bring to the table because that is the only way to lead in the midst of chaos. I don't know if you've ever watched surgery take place. There is a reason that surgeons are on the top of the medical food chain. They must learn the procedure from every angle in the room and be able to live it through the eyes, experience, and vocabulary of everyone present in that cold, sterile environment.

The surgeon is in complete command while at the same time completely dependent upon everyone in the room to do their part. There are times when he or she has to reorganize the room or ask a question. They must know enough about everyone else's job to ensure that when the unexpected happens, they maintain complete control and direct the energy of others toward a successful procedure and safe recovery for the individual. Every person centers around the surgeon and affords them a high level of respect because no matter how hard everyone else is working in the operating room, they know no one is working harder and with more at stake than the surgeon with the scalpel in his or her hand.

I feel the same about what I do. I work hard because I want to earn the respect of those who work for me. I want to know the details about every part of the organization so that I can direct the organization through the paths our MBOs afford us and, if necessary, redirect the organization in an entirely new direction. Just like the surgeon, my position as chief executive officer and founder places me in complete command while at the same time keeping me completely dependent upon everyone else to do their part.

chaos is not optional

Anyone who has spent any time at our international headquarters knows that the lifeblood of our organization is chaos. We don't take a long time to make decisions. We don't have a series of forms to fill out and hoops to jump through to start something new, stop something that doesn't work, or make adjustments along the way.

We had just moved into our new international headquarters. We relocated everyone, it seemed, overnight. Our relocation didn't need to result in any more downtime than necessary. Our organization is first and foremost about the people we serve, so they needed to know that our doors were open. But that meant that we would have to finish moving in along the way, an interesting challenge in and of itself.

Our conference room has glass doors. Just outside the doors is a board with feedback from a number of different people. Some have participated in a shoe drive, some have hosted an event, and others have received shoes. Some of the items hanging are pictures from children, hand-written notes from adults, and even news stories cut out and mailed to us. It's one of my favorite things in the office building.

The size of the board that we had was too small for all that we were receiving, so I hired a guy to come and make it bigger. It's outside our conference room because as we go in and out of meetings, I want everyone to be reminded of why we do what we do and to remember those with whom we are serving. We may only have a small number of employees, but our volunteer base is beyond belief.

So during a meeting, I looked up to see the contractor beginning his work. He was measuring, holding things up, and scratching his head. I was watching this through the doors and trying not to look too terribly distracted. We don't have many meetings, so the ones we do have are usually important. First he tried to add panels to the board that were close but didn't match. I politely excused myself from the meeting and requested that the panels match identically. Next, he tried to take down the existing board, which was about to tumble on top of him. I excused myself again and asked that he stop working until he talked to the project manager to be sure he knew what to do.

When I returned a second time, everyone had a smile on their face as they, too, had been watching this well-intentioned but confused worker try to complete this task. He didn't know how to complete this task any more than we who were sitting in the conference room did.

We've all been there. Any organization that moves as fast we do doesn't have time to perfect the process. The difference is that when we run into places and situations where we have never been, we should never "fake it until we make it." We should reach out to get help.

The same should be true for us. Chaos emerges as we raise children, advance in our career, and attempt to make a difference in the world. The goal is not to avoid chaos but to embrace it and use that energy to move you forward rather than hold you back.

chaos is Empowerment

Chaos is not optional for an organization, group, or individual trying to do something that matters. There will always be things along the way that distract us. We must know how to respond so that we remove any distractions and focus with an even greater intensity at accomplishing the task at hand. MBOs provide the structure needed to ensure the chaos that remains healthy and doesn't erode the very core of who we are and what we are trying to do.

Contrary to the opinion of many whom I've worked for and who have worked for me, you can operate a large organization without the bloated processes of one like the federal government. It shouldn't take weeks to order supplies, disburse funds, or implement and test a new idea. I become frustrated with anything that inhibits my ability to lead Soles4Souls due to senseless rules and regulations. Rules are meant to be stretched, and I love working with people who like to push the limits of what's possible. How else will we uncover the next game-changing strategy or initiative if we don't allow people to color outside the lines.

The brilliance of operating an organization using MBOs is that it helps focus others in a particular direction without prescribing each step to take. Soles4Souls has structure, but not so much that its environment is stifling. People who work for me are free to define new paths, set new courses, and rethink anything that is currently in place. As long as the idea is in line with a core MBO, then it is approved.

chaos makes world changers

Changing the world is not always pretty. It is full of victories and defeats. Its path is littered with the best of intentions from well meaning people who forgot why they started this fight to begin with. No one wakes up and says I want to change the world unless it is someone who is crazy enough to enjoy the blood, sweat, and tears that will come next.

Deciding to change the world begins by believing the way something is today is unacceptable and that standing by without interceding is not an option. Changing the world means placing more emphasis on getting it done than on getting it right.

At one point, I owned a boat. I love the water. It is one of the most peaceful places in the world. I remember this guy who had a slip next to mine. I always wondered why he always seemed to be on his boat every time I visited mine. He used to make fun of me because I would run out of gas and never could tie the boat to the dock in the proper way.

I told him one day that getting things perfect in life is less important than making a difference and enjoying the ride along the way. I needed time out on the boat to get away and think through an important conversation I had earlier that day. He never did accept me as a true captain of my ship, but I didn't care.

The pressures of being a leader can be overwhelming, so finding a few minutes away from everyone and everything can bring a lot of clarity to a situation. This is exponentially more important than making sure all the details are in place and to proper specification.

The same is true for a young child who decides to collect shoes for his or her birthday instead of receiving gifts. Or the young teenager who engages a school leader to allow them to use a day of school to work on community projects instead of papers. Or the college student who steps away from the expectations of Mom and Dad and charts a new path because of a moving experience or inspirational message. Or even a housewife who decides that while her children are in school she will start a blog or community group designed to make a difference in someone's life.

There are plenty of reasons why you could object to any of the ideas in this book. Life hands you a number of excuses not to do anything if it is too much work and requires too much sacrifice. All of it stems from a lack of certainty and fear of failure. What if you try to change the world and nothing happens? I want to challenge you to accept the chaos of life as the energy you will need to carry you forward as you allow the passion of your heart to direct you to make a difference in the life of another human being.

World changers don't have all the answers, but they have a burning passion to make an impact in a very specific way. World changers haven't discovered all the obstacles but feel the need is greater than any unanticipated roadblock. World changers aren't looking for a way to feel better about themselves but a way to spread light and joy in places that are dark and dreary.

TWELVE

Look out the windshield, not in the rearview Mirror

"Don't let yesterday use up too much of today."
—Cherokee Indian Proverb

For as many good decisions I've made in my life, I've certainly made a few bad ones too. I don't want you to walk away from this book thinking that I've figured it out or arrived. I've been hard on nonprofit leaders because I am one. I have high expectations for Americans who are, compared to the world's scale, wealthy in time, skill, and money because I find myself in that category.

What I can't understand is the general disinterest in getting dirty with the junk from the lives and tragedy of others when we are no different from the people who need our help.

In fact, we may be the very people in need. Just because we can dress up in nice clothes, live in big houses, and drive nice cars doesn't mean we aren't living in our own hell. Just because we have a particular skin color, live in a particular neighborhood, or have a limited education doesn't mean we don't have the capacity to make a difference in the lives of others that will live beyond our years on this earth.

There is a natural disaster happening in people's lives every day, and every day we must make a decision to either intercede and help or to ignore the situation believing someone else more qualified and better equipped will eventually come along. Whatever decisions we face, we must make choices again and again.

I don't know anything else to do but to push myself and others beyond our limits in hopes of reaching the next goal, the next threshold that allows all of us to have a bigger footprint and make a difference in more people's lives.

Dirty Feet

Your first trip outside the United States, especially to an impoverished country like Haiti, will change your perspective on life forever. One of our team members, after having just arrived in Haiti, began tearing up noticing the devastation almost immediately. I must admit that has been my reaction each and every time I land on Haitian soil.

There is always one person in the group traveling with Soles4Souls to distribute shoes who asks for a pair of gloves, for fear of getting dirty and touching uncertain substances. I completely understand their hesitation. The standard of living in Haiti is very different from ours, including their definition of cleanliness. Much of the reason for their living conditions is the lack of access to clean, running water and proper sewer systems, all of which was destroyed during the earthquake in January 2010.

I confess that I never wear gloves. Not because I'm not concerned about my own health. Not because there isn't something deep within my stomach that turns at the overbearing smell of a mixture of substances and the wonder of what it could be. I don't wear gloves because I want the child or individual I am fitting with a shoe to feel the human touch. There is something different about skin-on-skin contact that is difficult to describe and absolutely impossible to substitute.

Before we give them new shoes, we wash their feet. Nothing serves as a reminder of why Soles4Souls exists than when I am bent down in front of a child making his dirty feet clean. Some children are so young I wonder if anyone has ever washed their feet before.

I don't do this because I think it somehow qualifies me for some eternal destination. I don't do this because I want to feel better about myself. I do this because Mrs. Busch essentially did the same thing for me so many years ago.

She may never have knelt down and washed my feet, but she did tell me that I could do anything I wanted to in life. For a young man who felt hopeless, she gave me hope because she believed in me. That's why I wash dirty feet of children and adults around the world today. I want others to know the same hope that comes in the belief of a better tomorrow.

Today Matters

Some of the greatest excuses in life come from our inability to forgive ourselves of past mistakes. If only I had made this decision, taken this job, or chosen this career, then I could really make a difference. If only I had this much money, a little extra time, or more influence, then I could help others. Every day provides us with an opportunity to leave our excuses at the door of self-absorption and see the need and opportunity that exists within our neighborhoods, workplaces, and religious communities.

There is a reason that the largest window in a car is the windshield. When we drive, we look ahead to anticipate what's next. While it's important to mindfully look behind when anticipating a change, we don't drive forward with our eyes focused on what's happening behind us. Stop allowing the past to direct your future. Stop making excuses as to why you're not qualified, available, or suitable to help.

> **Some of the greatest excuses in life come from our inability to forgive ourselves of past mistakes.**

Whatever happened yesterday, happened yesterday. Our job is to learn from the past and move forward to the future. Determine what worked and what didn't so that you can make a better decision, a better investment, a greater difference today.

This is the easiest principle to discuss and the hardest to implement. Our natural tendency is to drift toward what is comfortable and what has proven to be successful while avoiding what seemingly failed in the past.

I'm at my best when I'm at the feet of others. The greatest task I have been commissioned to carry out is to be an ambassador to the hopeless, a voice for the voiceless, and a reminder about those who have been forgotten. I could make a million excuses as to why I could or should be doing other things, but I've chosen to ignore those excuses that quickly fade when you realize a small act of kindness to a stranger or close friend can change everything.

Too Many Have Given Up on Haiti

There is nothing I see, hear, or experience every time I land in Haiti that doesn't frustrate me and leave me with a burning desire to not give up on the Haitian people.

As I've had time to reflect on my experience, I'm greatly disturbed by a culture that is quick to rush into a country after a natural disaster, raise billions in a short period of time, and leave shortly after the last camera stops filming. What does that say about us?

Charity is not a new work or concept that developed in the American colonies. It's been around for centuries. In some respects, societies have viewed the poor as gateways to their own self-esteem rather than as equals. That's not right. The Haitian people deserve better from a country that possess the greatest wealth ever imagined in the history of the world.

Now, let's get one thing straight. I'm 100 percent capitalist, but our economy was built upon the common assumption that people would generally do the greatest good for the greatest number. When we lose our conscience it becomes all about us. Our entire recession came about as a result of our lost conscience. Too many people did what was best for them at the detriment of someone else.

I have a plan for Haiti. My plan is about establishing a new economy, not merely funneling more money to people in need. I want to help these people experience the joy of self-sustainment and the hope that comes as a result of it. However, I'm also committed to provide whatever relief I can until the baton can be passed and their new economy is in full swing.

The Fallacy of Success

I believe the reason so few people actually try to make a difference is because they fear failure. What if I try to help and it doesn't matter? What if, when I try, it becomes more than I can handle? What if I get hurt? What if I make the situation worse?

All of these questions are genuine, but none of them are worthy of taking yourself out of the game. The greatest lie we tell ourselves about success is that it is the opposite of failure. Not true. Some of the greatest successes in life are, in fact, the direct result of our greatest failures.

What turns our failures into success stories is our willingness to learn from what we experience and build on it. Soles4Souls is the organization it is because we're committed to failing fast and failing often. The people I know who are the greatest pictures of success are people fueled by their failures rather than stunted by them.

Perhaps the question we need to ask ourselves is, What if our decision, our investment, our risk turns out to be a huge success? What happens when a small act of kindness saves a life and that person goes on to help countless others. We will never fully understand the impact we can have on others, which is why we can't become consumed with our past. Rather, we must allow our past to remind us that we are completely human. It is our humanity that connects us, not our failures or our success.

Don't Be Fooled

We work really hard to look good on the outside. We attend the right colleges and universities. We earn degrees in the most promising fields. We look for the perfect internships and land the most coveted jobs. As a result, we are able to live in exclusive neighborhoods, drive fancy cars, and wear designer clothes.

No matter how good you look on the outside, you are no different from the hungry in India, the starving sister or brother in the Sudan, the homeless in Pakistan, and the devastated in Haiti. We are all human. We all have needs. Some have been given the opportunity to leverage the margin in their lives to make a lasting difference in the life of another.

We are no better than anyone else in spite of our best efforts to convince ourselves otherwise. The best we can hope for is an opportunity to change the life of another. The nightmare that should haunt us is hearing the cry of the helpless and finding ways to silence those voices with our own comforts.

The job of a nonprofit leader is to solve problems. Your job as a citizen of this world is to get involved. Nothing disqualifies you from the role that you are to play.

DO, Not Talk

I'm tired of people talking about their ideas. I'm weary of nonprofit leaders who recount again and again their best plans to do something wonderful. There is no amount of planning that matters if action doesn't follow. It's time to take what has been coming out of our mouths and put it into action. Stop talking. Start doing.

No matter who you are or what position you currently hold, you have the capacity to make a difference. However, you will never make a difference if all you do is sit around and talk.

Honestly, this is the frustration I have with Americans. We like to sit around and debate, pontificate, and get lost in the philosophy of economics, when the reality of the situation is that we need people to be reminded that we have a responsibility to each other. We must not forfeit our opportunity to help those in need or we risk finding ourselves alone in our time of need. This isn't socialism or communism; this is what it means to be human, connected, purposeful, and to live a life of meaning and significance.

Implement, Not Plan

I try to avoid meetings at all costs. I only attend meetings that are absolutely essential. Meetings, more often than not, postpone action instead of put things into motion. Haven't we had enough time to plan? Hasn't there been enough time wasted talking about moral obligations? Yes! It's time to roll up our sleeves, unbutton our collars, and get to work.

People tell me that they are waiting for a time later in their life or in their career when things are more stable and predictable to get involved in humanitarian efforts. I tell each and everyone one of them that the greatest sin against humankind is to place our own priorities above the needs of others.

We are not as important as we think we are. We are more prepared now than we'll ever be to make a difference in the lives of those around us. It's not only getting on a plane and traveling around the world, it's doing things like paying attention to the people in our lives who love us. Stop waiting for the right time. Do something now!

Show, Don't Tell

This is one of the greatest criticisms I have about religious communities today. There is a lot of telling but not enough showing. We are quick to listen to the respected teacher talk about the needy but unwilling to go into the alleys of our cities to offer food, water, shoes, and clothing to those people who have been beaten up by life.

The only difference between you and the homeless person you serve a meal to at the local shelter is that someone in your life cared about you enough to give you the strength to rise to the position of power and authority you have today. But you are not there to look down on other people. Rather, you are there to leverage your power, position, and authority to help others.

Open Your Eyes

There is much pain that surrounds us on any given day. Somewhere in the world today, someone is fighting to stay alive from lack of food, someone is dying from AIDS, someone is lying in a makeshift hospital with leftover drugs struggling to hang on just so they have the chance to say I love you one more time.

The need is great. Our time is now. We can either turn our back on humanity, or we can accept the fact that our knowledge of the need makes us responsible, our time makes us available, and our resources make us accountable to do something that matters instead of wasting our lives in the futile pursuit of fleeting pleasures.

The Promise of Tomorrow

"Look out the windshield, not in the rearview mirror" is a battle cry for those of us who want more out of life than what society says is important, valuable, and necessary. We are Americans, the greatest people in the world living in the greatest nation in the world. Make no mistake about it: our fortune comes with an obligation to share the promise of tomorrow with others.

We did not die on the battlefields of freedom to earn the right to absolve ourselves of the need to extend hope and help. This is our time. This is our moment. We must accept the notion that lingers deep within that there is more to this life than what we can earn or achieve. One day we will all die. Someone will bury us in the ground, and all that will be left will be a stone marker. Over time our names will be worn down by the weather. Our only chance at creating a lasting legacy is by reaching out and investing in the lives of those around us who need our smile, our touch, our insight, and our encouragement.

For some, the promise of tomorrow will carry you down the hall to reconnect with your teenager or across the street to an estranged neighbor. For some, the promise of tomorrow will carry you around the world to places that will never be tourist attractions, to meet people who will never make national headlines. Our willingness to offer promise for tomorrow affords us the strength and confidence in the providence of today.

The Power of Hope

When we realize the potential we have to do even bigger things than we might have first imagined, we can act with the boldness that only comes from hope. The greatest obstacle we have to overcome, which seems to cast a shadow of doubt over individuals and organizations trying to do something that matters, is the fear that we might not be the appropriate person or group to offer help.

Our lives are full of mistakes. Our pasts are cluttered with skeletons. Our personalities are clouded with imperfections. Still, none of that should hold us back from embracing the potential we have to offer hope to others. In light of our mistakes and personality flaws, we possess the power to give hope, life, and light to others. This is the divine nature that we can't explain, understand, or reproduce. It exists within each of us.

Look out the windshield, not in the rearview mirror. It's simple to say but hard to do. Those brave enough to follow through with this challenge will open themselves up to a dimension of existence that will change the world one person at a time.

We must become disturbed by our present condition before we are ready to admit that almost isn't good enough. We must forget the conventional before we can discover what is possible. This is the life that is possible for those who embrace the hope that is within.

Our gift to the world is not our presence nor our greatness. Our gift to the world is the choice to leave behind any reason or excuse we might cling to that would distract us from reaching into the depths of our own humanity, connecting with others, and demanding justice and mercy for all in light of the reality that almost is never good enough. Not now. Not ever.

conclusion:
The value of Human connections

The conclusion (my editor tells me) is supposed to review what has already been said. That means I'm not supposed to introduce any new ideas. Just for the record, I wanted a thirteenth chapter because I wasn't finished saying everything I wanted to say. However, the people in the publishing world are a bit superstitious. Any book ending with chapter 13 is out of the question.

I've pushed back enough on some other areas of the book that I feel it's best not to die on this hill. We did come to a compromise, which is why I'm writing this in what is officially being called the conclusion. Call it what you want, people like me (and maybe you) always flip to the end of the book to read a page or two and see if the book is worth reading. I was the one in school who flipped to the end of the chapter to read the questions first. That way I knew exactly what I should be focusing on so I could pass the test.

I don't want you to miss this next paragraph because it contains the substance and passion found in the sentences and paragraphs that fill the rest of the pages of this book.

Of all the things we have discussed, there is one thing upon which it all rests: the value of human connections. As humans, we are emotional beings. I know. I know. I've heard all the excuses too. I was a corporate executive, so I understand the discipline of making rational decisions. Yet I'm convinced that even the most rational people in the world are emotional.

A life void of emotion is really no life at all. We all operate within the dimension of our species that informs us beyond what we are able to calculate and quantify. It is best understood within relationships. There is no substitute for the connections we have with other people. There is a deep sense within each of us to identify and belong to a group, or even someone. The characters in the stories we tell each other again and again are those with whom we have connected. Those who have the richest stories also have the richest connections.

critic or convert

Some might read this book and think that I'm a slave-driving workaholic only interested in bottom line results and pushing the limits of my organization's capacity. Some might read this and see an ego-centric philanthropist who is only interested in building a monument to himself.

Say what you want. There have been plenty of critics who came to Soles4Souls only to be converted into raving evangelists. At no other time does this take place more consistently than when those who might think we have our priorities confused participate in, or even attend, one of our shoe distribution events. Perspectives change when the focus turns to the people we are working to help.

Critics will come and go. One way to easily spot them is to look on the sidelines. That's where they thrive. Few critics are able to remain that way after they get in the game. Why? Because connecting with other human beings makes the experience and the work real, personal, and full of emotion.

Convert isn't a word solely owned by the religious community. It describes an individual with a healthy dose of skepticism and cynicism who has discovered the substance of an organization is not in the financial balance sheet but in the depth of the human connection. I didn't decide at a young age to start Soles4Souls. It was a tug at my heart and a heaviness in my gut that directed me down the path to my life's work.

Take It Easy

I work hard. In fact, I would even say that I work harder now than I ever did as a corporate executive. But that doesn't mean I don't make time to play. One of the phrases that I use to diffuse a situation is, "Take it easy."

Sometimes I take my life too seriously. Perhaps we all do. This is why I love to spend time doing things that help me relax, whether that is having dinner with friends, playing cards, or riding my jet ski.

We should work hard. That's why they call it work. The temptation for those of us who live in the nonprofit world, though, is to think we can never relax. It's why the position of executive director has such a high turnover rate. It's why leaders of religious communities burn up and burn out.

The work we do to solve the social ills of the world is very serious business. We must be able to stay the course long enough to achieve a measurable difference. Therefore, we must take it easy from time to time and remind ourselves that love, passion, hope, and strength flow freely from us when we are rested and ready to serve others and strive to implement the strategies that will eliminate the problems we exist to solve.

Be Real

We have a "no voicemail" policy at Soles4Souls. What I mean by that is someone, a real person, is going to answer the phone. If by chance the person you are trying to get in touch with isn't available, the person who answered the phone will take a personal message.

There is nothing worse than calling an organization you hold in high esteem only to be treated as a pinball in a maze of automated menu options that eventually drop you into a general voicemail box.

Want to know a secret? I answer our phones too. Not because I have to, but because it is how I connect with the people who support and carry forward the work we are trying to do. I'm never too busy to talk to an individual or organization about Soles4Souls. Whether at a traffic light when driving a company vehicle or on the phone with an individual wanting to make a first-time donation, these are the very people who will help us reach our goal of giving away one pair of shoes every second.

Whatever you do in life, whatever position you hold, whatever level of achievement you rise to, never forget the secret to

Conclusion: The Value of Human Connections

success is being real with people. When you are who you are, you never have to remember who you pretended to be last.

We Are All the Same

There are three things that almost always change people: money, power, and position. The confusion sets in when we lose sight of the people we exist to serve and start seeing others as servants to us as we build our kingdoms. Those kingdoms might indeed be an entire sovereign nation or perhaps our personal homes.

My door is open. I answer the phones just like the receptionist in our office. I don't fly on a private, corporate jet. I am no different from the people who work for me, nor the people to whom we provide shoes.

I make mistakes. I sometimes say the wrong thing. And every now and then, I make a bad decision.

I say all of this to underline how odd it is to me that people talk to and about me as if I'm larger than life. Anyone and everyone has the opportunity to do something in life that matters and makes a difference in the lives of others. There is no special college degree that needs to be earned. There is no license that must be purchased. There is no membership fee that must be paid in order to qualify.

Don't let the comfort of your own life distract you from finding a place and a way to leave a legacy in the hearts and minds of people around the world. Don't let your age prevent you from thinking creatively about making an impact. Don't let geography or economics inhibit your willingness to go and be among people who are desperate for your affection and love.

We are all the same. We live within the same twenty-four hours. We are all given a certain number of years to walk this earth. We must discover the ways that are unique to our own giftedness, interests, and opportunity to give hope and help to others.

The Human Connection

My older brother, Timmy, was killed in a horrible traffic accident. He was a very good person who understood the value of the human connection. Part of why I do what I do is in honor of Timmy and his love for life and people.

I remember the funeral service as if it were yesterday. Everyone came up to me and said how sorry they were about my loss. I must have heard "I'm sorry" one thousand times that day. So many were incredibly kind and asked if there was anything they could do for me. I felt like so many people cared, more people than I had expected.

As the days went by, a good number of those who had first expressed concern and sympathies followed up. When the days became weeks, people were still faithful at checking in to see that I was OK, but the frequency of the calls and consistency of concern was coming from a shrinking group of people. As the weeks became months, the level of care and concern trickled down to almost no one who had originally made a promise to me that they would be there.

Six months after my brother's funeral, I was alone. Completely.

To this day I refuse to say "I'm sorry" in sympathy to anyone who has lost a loved one. Instead, I mark the date on my calendar and call them at least once a year to check in and follow up.

Every time I kneel before a man, woman, or child to wash their feet and give them a new pair of shoes, I wonder if they had experienced the same kind of loneliness that I had. Did they feel forgotten and overlooked?

Today, there is someone who needs a voice.

Today, there is someone who needs love.

Today, there is someone who feels forgotten and alone.

That someone isn't too far from where you are. When we stop seeing people who don't look like us, drive the same cars we drive, or live in the same neighborhoods we live in as nameless, faceless statistics, we begin to see others for who they are, human beings who deserve to be cared for, loved, and never left alone.

Mrs. Busch unleashed within my life the potential to do things some people only dream about. I want to do the same for you.

Open your heart.
Open your eyes.
Open your ears.

Only then will we be in a position to receive the gift that comes through the human connection. And such a gift demands much more than our best intentions. In the face of the hurting, the poor, and the forgotten, almost simply isn't good enough—and it never will be.